INTRIGUE

Don Carey

Don Carey
2019.

COUNTRY BOOKS

Published by Country Books
Courtyard Cottage, Little Longstone, Bakewell, Derbyshire DE45 1NN
Tel: 01629 640670
e-mail: dickrichardson@countrybooks.biz
www.countrybooks.biz
www.sussexbooks.co.uk

ISBN 978-1-910489-67-3

CHAPTER ONE

The man waited for his bill with ill concealed impatience, finished his wine and pushed back the chair which grated sharply on the stone floor. The noise startled the waiter, who hastily scribbled out *l'addition* and apologetically proffered it to the tall stranger who peeled off a number of euro notes and left as silently as he had arrived.

The night air was cool and a light breeze ruffled the emerging leaves of the plane trees. He pulled up the collar of his jacket and made his way across the empty street and passed the silent fountain with its faded war memorial. Out of habit he glanced at the artificially lit window of the estate agents with its optimistically priced properties and turned down the unlit narrow lane. With the aid of a watery moon he made his way to the bottom of the hill and stopped outside the heavy oak door which led to his temporary home.

The shot that killed him came from a small calibre silenced rifle expertly fired from the top of the lane. No cartridge was found but the angle of the bullet entry cast no doubt where the killer had been standing. After six months of lack lustre enquiry the French police closed its file.

CHAPTER TWO

Richard liked the village. Had anyone told him years ago that he would end up retiring to a quiet Hampshire retreat and enjoying it he would have laughed with incredulity. But the years of stress and subterfuge had taken a mental as well as a physical toll and the total exhaustion compelled a life change.

He looked without seeing the rain dripping off the thatched roof and a myriad of thoughts chased themselves across his brain. He thought he would be intensely lonely in his new life and from time to time he was, but with the loneliness came cherished privacy. While he welcomed the peace such privacy brought he recognised the danger of too much introspection and forced himself to socialise, albeit among villagers who themselves were not known to being extrovert.

He had made a good friend of his newly appointed G.P., a relaxed fifty-something doctor with a quirky sense of humour and a healthy perspective of life and human weaknesses. His profession demanded confidences that Richard would normally have been uncomfortable to give but these had been respected and Richard respected the man.

"Never forget that old age will bring its own problems," Peter had said at one of their first meetings, "and when you spend more time remembering the past than looking forward to the future then you are already old."

So Richard was already old. In truth his memories offered a reflective excitement not easily repeatable in the life he could see ahead of him. He did not fear the future but rather faced it with curiosity and equanimity.

"Lucky chap, Richard," smiled the Chairman of the Board at his farewell drinks party, "Time to do all those things you have always wanted to do but never got round to, eh?"

Richard responded with a weak smile. David was the same age as he with a small fortune beckoning as a pension in some two years time together with the inevitable knighthood. Richard did not think David had ever understood the real world nor needed to bother with it, come to that.

His thoughts drifted to the second meeting of the day which was possibly more significant. The surroundings could hardly have been of greater contrast; they sat in a non-descript café within the grey arches of Villiers Street close to Charing Cross. He had only met the man once before and knew that he would never see him again. He did not know his name and had not asked.

"Your daughter is doing very well. You will be able to see more of her now."

Of course he knew his daughter; that was the link.

"Possibly, I may travel though. I haven't thought it through."

"No, but be careful. Retirement is not always as enjoyable as one would hope. Anyway, thank you!"

"What for?"

"Oh, everything. The Office doesn't show much in the way of gratitude but you have been a great help."

"I am not sure entirely how or why."

"No, of course not, but we also think you may be of some use in your new life. Just keep your eyes and ears open, and take care."

"Of course," said Richard and he knew it was pointless to ask for any explanation.

"Well, I must be getting on." With that the featureless man in the slightly shabby grey suit made to get up from his chair, but paused to say one more thing.

"And Richard, do remember that you are still bound by the Official Secrets Act."

*   *   *

The rain had stopped and the sun made a brave effort to relieve the gloom. Richard could never work out whether he really liked England in March. He accepted the rigours of winter but in his view the weather should, by the time the clocks went forward, show some signs of improvement. He heaved himself to his feet, struggled into his outdoor clothes and summoned the dog from his comfortable basket.

"If I can put up with it, so can you," he grunted at the golden retriever who wagged his tail in glorious anticipation of an unexpected walk.

As Richard walked he thought about the life he had left behind him and the strange meeting with his erstwhile contact. He knew little about the grubby world with which he had unwittingly been brought into contact many years before. In a simplistic way he had initially believed that the little tasks he had been asked to carry out were both in the national interest and by definition, morally supportable. As the years passed his cynicism grew exponentially and he no longer questioned the morality of it all. To do so would have given him discomfort; a problem to be resolved at some time, but not now.

As with religion. When he was ten he sang in the church choir without believing or disbelieving the concept of God. Six years later he was filled with religious fervour but only two years after that he embraced the agnostic views of his peers. Mid-life sowed the seeds of doubt about either extreme view and as time went on he recognised his own mortality and realised that he still had no answer to what was becoming an uncomfortable dichotomy.

The shout came from somewhere near the hedgerow and he turned to see his retriever trying to bound between the tractor furrows and wag his tail at the same time, recognising Tom Wakefield from the pub. Tom always had biscuits in his jacket pockets for encounters such as these, of which Buster was fully aware.

"Settling in then?" Tom asked the same question each time they had met over the past six months and Richard now recognised that he would be a newcomer for many months to come.

"Sort of," had now become the traditional answer. Tom was a farmer's labourer, in his thirties, with a ruddy face which came from his work in the blustery outdoors or from enjoying the free pints which came from his part-time job. Richard was not sure which.

"How's the pub getting along?" questioned Richard, mainly out of something to say.

"Not bad," said Tom, "we do good trade from the folks at the top of the village particularly on a Friday lunch-time. Reckon they try to work only half a day, that lot!" he chuckled, "Still they're O.K. – keep themselves to themselves, that's for sure."

"What does it do – the firm, I mean?"

"Not really sure, something to do with electronics, I think, but I've never heard them talk any business in my hearing, so I can't properly say."

"No. Well, must be getting on!" Richard called his dog away from the cowpats which Buster considered a prime delicacy; apparently and curiously not to the taste of humans.

The sun seemed to be resisting its imminent disappearance over the horizon with an awesome display of burning fury as its rays lit up the still clouds which promised a better day to follow the night. There was no warmth from its presence for it was March when the sun would set within the hour. Richard stood admiring the majesty of the moment and thought this was the England he cherished, with rolling countryside still shaking itself dry and offering a solitude to those who could give time to saviour its silence and beauty.

He knew he had come home.

*   *   *

"Did someone see Merrington?" The grey haired man quizzed his associate who was studying a very in-complete Telegraph crossword.

"Oh that, yes, no problems there. All set up for a happy retirement in the bowels of the Hampshire countryside. Give it a year and he will be as bored as hell!"

"I'm not so sure," said the senior man thoughtfully, "that South African business nearly took him apart last time and then losing the girl. I am not surprised he wanted to get away from it all."

"Maybe. At least he never found out how much we were involved. Though he is no fool and he must have had his suspicions."

"Of course. Fancy a beer and a sandwich?"

The two disparate men strolled along the Embankment in the spring sunshine, each immersed in his own thoughts. Geoffrey Dawson, the elder of the two, wistfully considered his own retirement which, by definition would have to be discreet and to a large extent, anonymous. Such was the penalty of his job. Many times he had yearned for the freedom to declare himself to the world; to show his strengths and weaknesses and even join the commuters in their five-o'clock crush to get home. But it was not to be and he had to be thankful for the more than adequate salary and the possibility of an OBE. He shook his head and concentrated on the sights and sounds of an April day in London where the sun was shining and the girls were looking exceptionally pretty.

In contrast Neil was thinking about Richard Merrington, the nearly disgraced business man who had had a chequered career but now deserved the tranquillity of a country retirement. He had proved to be a useful and reliable agent in a world as far removed as it could possibly be. A chance remark by Jan on the Polish desk had led him to contact her father who had by reason of the background search on Jan when she was first employed passed all the security checks necessary.

In any event the engagement had been a need-to-know and a now-and-again basis which suited them both. On a number of occasions Richard had acted as the unwitting messenger to other contacts in the field but he had asked no questions even though he might well have been putting himself in danger.

Now Neil wondered if he could use Richard on the Mougins affair, as it had become known in the Office. The man who had been killed had not been important but his death represented a demeaning insult to '5', even disallowing the human tragedy of it all; and so utterly pointless, or so it had seemed.

"I'm thinking of using Richard Merrington on the Mougins job," he said.

Geoffrey stopped, looked at Neil and then beckoned him to join him at the concrete barrier overlooking the Thames. Westminster Bridge to their right was already crowded as office workers jostled with Japanese and their cameras endlessly shuttering their presence.

"I never cease to admire the London Eye," said Geoffrey, "I used to think of it as an eyesore but it's grown on me now."

"Did you know it takes thirty minutes for each revolution and can carry eight hundred people at a go?" asked Neil, "what a terrorist target!"

"Thank you Neil, and yes I am aware of all the facts as indeed are others in the Office. Now on the subject of Merrington, do you really think he is up to it?"

"Depends what "it" is. We've got nothing to go on except that one small time casual agent has been killed who had limited information which would have been of precious little use to anyone and the trail has gone cold. Presumably it was a contract killing but by whom and to what purpose?"

"So why do you think Merrington would be of any value?"

"Firstly," said Neil, warming to his theme, "he is not involved in any circuit so has no profile. Secondly he no longer has any business ties of any consequence, thirdly he is probably bored stiff and fourthly if he screws up it will not come back to us."

"And what about his daughter?"

"She's been around for quite a while now and knows the score. Besides if she doesn't like the consequences she shouldn't have put his name forward in the first place."

"God alive; you are a sympathetic sod, Neil. O.K., Merrington it is, but we are totally off record. Will you look after this personally, Neil?"

"Of course. I assume that I have the authority to agree all arrangements and expenses?"

"Don't ask damn fool questions. I told you – this one is off record – whatever you do is down to you and, subject to regular de-briefings, no one else. Do we understand each other?"

"Of course Geoffrey. If I screw it up and spend a large slice of the

Firm's income in doing so then I am the one for the chop."

"Something like that, old boy, something like that."

*   *   *

The Norman church at the end of the village had always fascinated Richard. Why, he was uncertain but in a way it seemed to set itself apart from the quiet smugness and faux superiority of the comfortable houses by which it was surrounded. It was as if the church exuded an unforgiving atmosphere which in turn made him feel slightly uncomfortable.

It was not, he thought, his conscience showing guilt at the infrequencies of his attendance; he had few qualms on that score. Rather it was as if the church put up with its visitors out of sufferance in the knowledge that too many believed their attendance was necessary to emphasize their status in the village. The church lacked warmth, not just in its ambient temperature, but in its very welcome. To Richard it still played homage to the 12th Century nobility who were in the main its parishioners at the time.

He had determined one day to explore fully the church and its precincts but Buster resisted going beyond the entrance gates with uncharacteristic stubbornness and whimpering, which to Richard's mind was due to fear of the burial grounds.

Today, though, it was a damp Friday and he had left Buster in the warmth of his kitchen to set out for the church. He walked purposefully through the village, past the pub and past the old school house. He met no-one, although the occasional house had its lights burning even though it was still afternoon.

His imagination played tricks with him, for he felt the mist of the grey afternoon closing in on him as he walked up the short path and the unseasonal coldness seemed more intense, causing him to shiver. The graves on either side looked down on him, for the centuries of dead souls within had caused the land to be some five feet above the level of the path. He was glad to push open the heavy oak door and gain the inner sanctuary of the church.

For all its history the church held little charm for him and Richard soon tired of the grey stones walls and the silent pews. He made his way out to the church yard and like any tourist examined the worn headstones which could still be deciphered.

These did little to dispel his gloom as they showed all too clearly the shortage of life expectancy in those early days.

Richard shook his head as if to free his being from the depression which threatened, but before he left he wandered around the back of the church where, it seemed, any headstones had long been removed leaving mounds of grassy earth as the only evidence of past sadness. He turned oh his heel and as he did so caught a glimpse of marble tucked away discreetly in a small corner alongside the church wall. It was indeed a headstone, but not old or weathered. He read the short inscription

'Frederick Carol ("Freddy")
1974 – 1994.
In Remembrance'

Richard studied the grave for some time but then turned away as his depression threatened to return.

A light breeze had cleared away the damp mist and there was now warmth in the April sun, which lightened both his surroundings and his spirits. With some regret he walked past the pub as he would have enjoyed a pint but not, he told himself sternly, at four o'clock in the afternoon.

Now that the mist had cleared the village people were emerging on to their gardens and the street. Some he knew to wish them well, others he either knew by sight but not by name. Time will take care of that, he decided.

"You look lost in thought, Richard," said Peter, tapping him on the shoulder, "as if you had lost a pound and found a penny, as my father used to say!"

"Indeed," smiled Richard, "except nowadays a penny scarcely exists."

"Quite so; I suppose it will be bitcoins in the future. Anyway, may I introduce my daughter? Sian, this is Richard; a relative newcomer to the village and a welcome addition."

He could see the likeness between father and daughter, she was good looking rather than pretty, as tall as Peter but willowy where he was stocky. She was probably in her late twenties or early thirties, he thought, and above all she had an attractive smile.

"My pleasure," he smiled, "I like your name."

Her laugh was as attractive as her smile: "It could have been a lot worse," she said, "when I was born my parents couldn't think of a proper name and for three months I was called Poppy! Imagine growing up with that!"

"Sian is just down for a long weekend," explained Peter, "she comes down now and again just to make sure her old man is not up to any mischief. As if..." he said, a little wistfully.

Richard knew the doctor was living on his own but not whether he was a widower or divorced. In that sense he always kept himself very much to himself.

They chatted amicably as they made their way though the village; inconsequential stuff about this and that, light frothy and most enjoyable.

"Peter, there is something I want to ask you," said Richard. "I decided to look around the church for something to do."

"I am sure the Almighty will be very pleased about that. And?"

"And I came across a fairly new headstone round the back of the church. Tucked away and on its own. Any other headstones in that area had long been removed so I was curious. A young man of only twenty called 'Freddy Carol'. Ring any bells?"

"No idea, Richard. Churchyards are not really my thing, you know. It is my job to look after the living and delay their place in the churchyard for as long as possible. Sorry, but you could ask Tom – he should know."

"Tom – you mean Tom at the pub? I thought he worked at a farm during the day and the pub in the evening?"

"He also acts as a part time postman, an odd job builder and mows the church grass. If he doesn't know, he will be able to find out."

"Are you always called Richard?" Sian's eyes twinkled when she laughed. "Why not, for example, Dick?"

"I have been called 'Dick' in my time," he said, "But it had certain connotations that could be said to be a little rude; indeed on some occasions they often were. So I have always been 'Richard' to my friends."

The thought of a welcoming pint stayed with him until six o'clock, which he thought was not an unreasonable time to quench a thirst.

"Hello, Dick," Tom called out cheerfully from behind the bar, "Haven't seen you for a while and certainly not at this time! Nice to have company I must say. It is like a morgue in here until gone seven."

"Which reminds me, Tom. I want your help on a small matter. Join me in a pint?"

"Don't mind if I do! Two pints coming up"

So he told Tom about his trip to the church and the discovery of the isolated headstone.

"Word has it that amongst other things you look after the churchyard. Do you know the grave I am talking about?"

"No idea at all. Didn't even know it was there. I only cut the grass at the front to keep it tidy for the Sunday lot. Never been round the back. But does it occur to you that churchyards are where they bury people? It's been the practice for some years, so they tell me!"

Tom laughed at his own joke that he thought was one of the best he had heard in a long while.

"Yes, Tom, I did know that. But I've only been down here for a short while and I'm still learning my way around. But isn't there an overspill churchyard just outside the village?"

"Certainly there is. The one at the church is full to overflowing. They don't bury people there now you know. Oh! I see what you mean! What was the date on that gravestone?"

"1994. Freddie Carol."

"Curious," said Tom, "very curious. I'll ask around. Someone will know."

"If you would Tom, thanks. And it's Richard, not Dick."

CHAPTER THREE

"You've made contact with Merrington before" said Neil. "I want you to be the case officer on the Mougins affair reporting directly and only to me. I repeat – only to me. Understood?"

"Perfectly," replied the man, "I have read all the reports. Is there anything I should hold back on when I talk to him?"

"No, as long as you stick to the facts and don't introduce any views or guesswork. There are few enough facts to go on anyway. We want to fill in any gaps and decide if we take it any further. I hate blank walls."

*   *   *

Richard Merrington was decidedly cross. He had thought that he had successfully cut all his ties and could sit in the quiet English countryside in grand isolation, if that was to be his choice. Not so, it seemed.

The Manager at the bank had of course been courtesy itself when he telephoned. Richard had known him for a number of years and he had been one of the few people to whom he had entrusted his contact details after he had moved. He had also made it crystal clear that he did not expect to be disturbed, except in an emergency.

"Sorry, Richard but we have a problem with your new Will. We are a bit stuck and it's not something we can sort out long distance. Normally of course I would come and visit you personally but I honestly don't know when I could fit you in, is there any chance you could pop in next week? I may even be able to organise a lunch for you."

*   *   *

Surprisingly the train pulled into Waterloo on time and Richard made his way to the taxi rank at the back of the station. At mid–morning there were many more taxis waiting than there were people who needed them, and indeed the taxi queue stretched as far as the eye could see, each with its orange light futilely advertising the cab's availability.

"Bloody Uber" said the cabbie aggressively. "Not one of then would even pass the Knowledge. Don't suppose the new Mayor will do anything about it either!" he added gloomily.

They drove across Waterloo Bridge with its new cycle lane which guaranteed freedom for cyclists and traffic jams for the rest.

"Boris's legacy," said the driver, "be a nice idea if they could charge them all with road tax, like all of us motorists"

Richard was becoming marginally irritated by the cabby's aggression to the world at large.

"Hang on a minute," he said, "for all you know I'm a keen cyclist!"

"Not you guv, not with your suit and tie and the fact that you are prepared to pay my high fare just to get across Waterloo Bridge! Nah, – but I could be wrong," he added brightly, "it has been known!"

The Strand was grid-locked from one end to the other so Richard decided to dispense with the aggravating taxi driver and keep the fare to a single figure by dismounting at the corner of the Strand. For once it was not raining and the day was pleasant enough. He soon tired of the jostling crowds which seemed to fill every available pavement space and he was glad to cross the street by wending through the immobile traffic and entering the imposing glass doors to the bank.

He flicked idly through the Financial Times as he waited in the reception area, with only a solitary goldfish in the ornamental pool for company.

"Richard, my dear chap! How good to see you!"

Jeremy Sutcliffe was, thought Richard, the epitome of a bank manager. Immaculately dressed in a crisply starched white shirt and a somewhat dated three piece suit, the picture would have been straight out of "Esquire" had he also worn a watch and chain across his expanse of waistcoat.

"Absolute privilege to see you in this neck of the woods." burbled Jeremy as he ushered his visitor to the lift,. "We are in Room 7, I believe."

Followed by Richard he manoeuvred his way along the soulless corridors and past the identical conference rooms chatting inconsequentially as he went. He held the door open for Richard to enter Room 7.

"Do come in Richard won't you? I believe you have already met Mr Smithson?"

And the man in the shabby grey suit turned to shake the hand of Richard Merrington.

The banker had quietly left the room shutting the door behind him. Merrington tried not to show the astonishment he felt and to cover his confusion said:

"I never did know your name. Mr Smithson, is it?"

The corner of Smithson's mouth puckered in a half-smile.

"If you like. It will do for today."

"I see – how do the bank get involved?"

"They don't really, but we meet with Mr Sutcliffe from time to time. Rather like we do with you."

"Did," emphasised Richard. "I am not aware of any ongoing relationship. Probably a silly question in the circumstances, but why all this cloak and dagger stuff?"

"As you say, probably an unnecessary question. We are quite interested in continuing our previous relationship, subject of course, to you sharing in that interest."

Richard listened intently to Smithson as he spoke

"Mougins is a village 15 kilometres north of Cannes in the south east of France. Our agent was a forty year old English national with a dual passport living at Biot, a small commune ten kilometres to the north-east of Mougins, and was shot as he was entering his holiday home on Wednesday 9th March 2017 at approximately 2100 hours, local time. The post mortem established that he was killed by a ·308 rifle bullet which entered his back and severed the dorsal scapular artery, Death was virtually instantaneous. Apart from his identity papers and 300 euros in notes no further items were found on his body.

"Although he was only a casual agent we need to close the file on him. There was no apparent motive, no one has claimed responsibility. He paid his holiday rental in full for two weeks' stay and appeared to pay for all his outgoings by cash. He had been in occupation for seven days.

"The body was discovered by a near neighbour the following morning. The French police contacted the British Embassy which in turn notified us. The man had no known living relatives and appeared to be a total loner without any known friends or acquaintances. The Embassy, with our agreement, arranged for his cremation and disposal of ashes. The police were instructed to close their file."

"By whom?" Richard interjected.

Smithson looked at him intently and, after a pause, "Mr Merrington I am instructed to tell you everything you reasonably need to know about this case. You do not need to know the answer to that question."

"Understood" said Richard, slowly, "but I have yet to be told why you think I could be involved and I have yet to decide whether I will agree. I need to know a lot more before I decide!"

*   *   *

Of course he had agreed, as they knew he would. They knew more about him than was comfortable. They knew his strengths, his weaknesses, his foibles, his loneliness and the emptiness of his life. That he spoke passable French, had no living immediate relatives apart from his daughter and that he could not easily forego a challenge. Two weeks on holiday in the south of France with all expenses paid, with a wide ranging mandate to find out anything he could with no recriminations if he made no progress – of course he had agreed.

He gazed out of the train window, deep in contemplation. The lunch partially offered by Jeremy Sutcliffe as a bribe had not of course materialized. So he had found his way back to the shabby café in Villiers Street where he had last met "Mr Smithson" and had a cappuccino which washed down a tired looking bun before making his way back to Waterloo.

In his mind's eye he analysed not only what he had been told but also what he had not. He now knew the name and date of birth of the dead agent, that he had worked for the Office on a casual basis supplying in the past some sort of information but he had no idea what it contained nor how regularly he had made contact. As an agent he would have had a code name, but that was not for him to know.

Apparently the man had flitted around the coastal towns offering water colours for sale to the tourists ("and they were not at all bad," admitted Smithson) but had no other visible means of support. He had no close friends and no known relatives

"... but he had some interesting sources of information" said Smithson enigmatically, before politely refusing to elaborate.

So, no motive, no clues, no ideas. Great! With that Richard Merrington closed his eyes and thought of nothing until he woke up at Winchester station.

CHAPTER FOUR

Sian enjoyed visiting rural England, as she liked to call it, but her enthusiasm was less emphatic from October to March. She failed to see the attraction of Hampshire village life when it was dark at five o'clock and inevitably raining or at least broody and depressing. She therefore managed, without giving offence, to limit the visits to her doctor father only twice during the winter months plus the odd Christmas. The arrangement suited them both and they were both looking forward with equal pleasure to the warm weather and light summer walks in each others' company.

Sian had a deep friendship with her father, for they understood each other and the need to lead their separate lives in their own individual ways without confusing their relationship with unnecessary displays of affection or intrusion.

She turned off the farm track and into the cool shade of the overarching trees where they naturally formed a wide avenue of graceful beauty.

Sian loved it here. The earth beneath her feet was a carpet of softness made up from the fallen leaves inter-woven with moss and crumbled remnants of dead branches and twigs. Even the birds seemed to respect this place with only an occasional call to a friend or neighbour. The sun dappled its way into the glade with a quiet gentleness as it would into a church, for that, in its way, is what it was. Once she had seen a deer motionless in the shadows, not even disturbed by her presence.

Her thoughts turned to her father and his apparently lonely existence. Yet, he seemed happy enough, certainly compared to his life ten years ago.

At the time she had only recently come down from a provincial university with a modest 2·2 in English History. What she was going to do with her degree she had not the faintest idea which marginally bothered her and certainly worried her parents.

More accurately it worried her father, a busy general practitioner working out of the local hospital, mainly because he wanted her to be happy and to forge a promising future or a successful marriage, neither of which at the time seemed very likely.

Her relationship with her mother was at the best guarded. A small bird-like woman with a propensity to annoy, she offered little warmth to either her husband or daughter. Sian having experienced a taste of freedom while on campus found it difficult to adjust and decided to travel the world, picking up jobs when she could, in the time honoured student way.

She was in Australia when her father phoned. Her mother at the age of forty-eight had been diagnosed with a brain tumour and within months she was dead, against all medical forecasts.

"As you were planning to return to England in the near future, I saw no reason to contact you earlier," he said. "The consultant had given her a year to live."

Sian could well understand her father's shock and stress but there was something else, something intangible. His depression and anxiety did not abate for the next three months and he took to drinking to an excessive degree.

Then, one night after supper, he started talking; firstly to himself as if to give himself confidence and then to Sian. Unusually he only had two glasses of wine during the whole meal and now talked lucidly and with purpose.

"I'm sorry Sian. I am sorry to have been so selfish over these last few months. Your mother's death has hit me very badly."

"There's no need to apologise Dad. People deal with grief in different ways. I knew you would pull through but I am relieved that you can now talk about it."

"No, Sian you don't understand – but then how could you? I've never told you but I feel I caused Mum's death and that is a difficult cross to bear. I wasn't sure I could make it but having you has helped enormously."

"Dad, I've hardly helped. I've fed you and worried about you but I just felt so inadequate. I have been grieving too but it hasn't hit me to the same extent. I was never that close to Mum."

"No, I know. She was not an easy person to love. Perhaps I should not say this to you but ours was a difficult marriage, I am afraid the love element had long since disappeared – but that was no excuse."

"No excuse for what Dad? I don't understand."

"No, of course" he hesitated and was quiet for some time and she wondered whether he would or could continue. Then slowly "I had an affair, Sian. I had an affair and I told your mother about it. I think it killed her."

*   *   *

She had reached the end of the forest glade and turned onto a narrow track which ran along the side of a newly sown cornfield. There she stopped, looking at the buzzard circling high up, searching for its prey while she relived her life and that of her father's.

She could not find it in herself to criticise or condemn her own father. Surprised, yes, but he was not the first man to stray and certainly not the last. In a way it showed a strength of character that she had not suspected in this most amiable of men and while what he had done had possibly been morally insupportable, in a curious sort of way she wanted to cheer him from the sidelines.

So she set off once more on her travels, had an intense affair with an Italian which lasted most of the summer and when it finished had a one night stand with an itinerant Englishmen as if to prove something to herself. After which she took a dispassionate look at her lifestyle and returned to her small flat in Bayswater and a routine job with a travel agent. By then her father had sold the family home and taken a job as a part time locum at the village surgery and established a small local private practice.

Not for the first time, thinking of her father made her wonder if she could contemplate living nearer to him. Not with him but nearer to him. She had a reasonable bank balance thanks to the mother's bequest and the delights of Bayswater had long since passed her by while her job was excruciatingly tedious. The countryside had an irresistible charm even in the winter, when contrasted with city pave-ments.

She could understand why her father had found a quiet contentment in village life and being a doctor meant that he was soon involved in local life and had made some good friends.

Whether she could do the same was another matter but she had begun to think more positively of late. She would meet people and make friends she was sure. "After all," she thought to herself, "there was that rather dishy Richard Merrington. I've always been attracted to older men. In any case, if I fancied a bit of rough there is always Tom at the pub!"

With which lascivious thought she arrived back at her father's door.

*   *   *

The subject of Sian's semi-erotic thoughts was at that moment wiping clean the bar counter and polishing glasses for the evening session. At five o'clock in the afternoon he had not expected to be disturbed but the knocking at the door was too insistent to be ignored and the apologetic visitor was a young, diffident man seeking accommodation for the night.

"Not up to me," Tom explained. "I only work here part time but from what I see there should be no problem. Come back in about two hours and I will have checked it out, Not local are you?"

"Oh no, it's just that tomorrow I'm starting a two month contract up the road, I thought I'd come down a little early to get the lie of the land if you see what I mean. Hopefully they will have made some arrangement for me, maybe even here, but I won't know until tomorrow."

"No problem, if I can have your name?"

"Yes, of course, Williams, Stefan Williams. About 7pm then?"

"Yes, I'm pretty sure it will be O.K. My name is Tom, by the way."

Tom had put the slightly odd conversation he had had with Dick Merrington on one side until now, but now he might be able to dig deeper.

CHAPTER FIVE

Nice had always has a unique appeal to Richard. The warmth of the summer months and the indefinable atmosphere of the bars and restaurants were attractions, of course, but of a superficial nature. Rather it was the backcloth of past experiences, some sad, some less so which meant he was returning to the welcome of an old friend.

"Ten minutes to landing," said the disembodied co-pilot, "the temperature in Nice is twenty-three degrees and it is very sunny. Sorry we will be some thirty minutes late but it's better to arrive late than be dead on time!"

Which may either raise a smile or be considered as black humour, thought Richard. Possibly not the best line for someone angling for promotion.

He looked out of the port side windows as the 747 swept the Mediterranean and established its landing approach and the memories briefly returned, only for some to be put back firmly in their box. Memories were the reminiscences of old age and he was not there yet. Not quite.

He did however remember a few days spent at about this time of year. The death of his wife had shattered him both physically and mentally and he had struggled to drag himself back into the real world. Well meaning friends had urged him to take a break, away from it all, away from the condolences and false bonhomie and the efforts made to restore his sanity.

It was May, as it was now, and the idea of the anonymity of a foreign city and the therapy of spring sunshine had appealed. He had asked the travel agent to make the arrangements; the hotel was reasonable and the room adequate but over the three days the rain had been unrelenting. He sat on the edge of his bed staring out at the hotel swimming pool, its surface constantly agitated by the endless pounding of rain from a grey over-laden sky as tears ravaged his face. He could not forget.

Disembarking into the warm sunshine in a cloudless sky banished that memory for now and Richard collected his case from the baggage hall, changed his sterling notes for euros and walked through the customs hall staffed by patently disinterested officials. The public concourse was crowded with drivers displaying the name of their intended passengers. As always the taxi firm had mis-spelt his name but he recognised the driver and within half an hour was at the hotel.

"Bienvenue Monsieur Merrington. J'ai réservé votre chambre préférée."

He smiled at the dark haired girl.

"Hello Feena, your French puts me to shame I can't even detect an Irish brogue this time, you have obviously settled in well enough. How are things?"

"Better now, thank you," quietly, her face softening. He remembered now that by tacit agreement none of the staff would ever talk about the evening of terror so many months ago.

He booked into his room, unpacked and walked into the late spring sunshine from the hotel foyer and on to the Promenade des Anglais. Unsurprisingly the broad pave-ment was almost deserted. No young lovers holding hands and laughing to the world. Few fitness fanatics forever glancing at their wrist watches or cyclists aggressively ringing the bells at innocent pedestrians. This was not the Nice he had known, nor in his view would it ever be so again.

He stopped by the carpet of flowers and messages which covered the place where death had visited young and old, all eighty-six of them on Bastille Day in 2016. Like many others he inwardly raged at the stupidity and inhumanity of it all. He recalled a quotation: "Sin bought death and death will disappear with the disappearance of sin."

He turned on his heel and strode away from the place so that none could see his tears.

He inserted the hotel card and walked into Room 501, which he knew so well. His suitcase, along with his cabin bag had already been delivered. He turned off the air condition-ing, pulled back the curtains and pushed open the sliding doors separating his room from the patio.

The May sun had lost something of its intensity and he sat on one of the patio chairs and looked out at the Baie des Anges with its more determined sun-bathers sprawled across the pebbly beach. Violence in such an idyllic haven seemed almost incom-prehensible and certainly obscene.

Such a thought jerked Richard back to reality and the reason for his visit. He fetched what little information the office had considered could be released to him:

RESTRICTED CIRCULATION: CATEGORY 'A' U.K. EYES ONLY

Name:	John Michael VINCE.
Born:	5 August 1977, Dover, Kent, U.K.
Died:	9 March 2017, Mougins, France.
Mother:	Jane VINCE (Spinster)
Father:	No details shown.
Last known address:	14(a) Rue de L'Inconnu, Biot, Provence-Alpes-Cote d'Azur, France.
Education:	1987-1993 Dover Grammar School for Boys. Member CCF. GCSE Certificate: English, French, Maths, History, General Science.
Career:	1993-1995 Paid Police Cadet, Kent Police. 1995-1997 Police Constable, Met. Police 1997-2000 Police Tactical Unit. 2000 Resigned. 2000-2017 Occasional Agent.
Agent Number & Code	Redacted.
Agent Activities:	Redacted.

Note: re Jane Vince: Born 1958, Dover, Kent. Moved to Battersea, London August 1993. Unmarried. Died May 1995 in childbirth. No details of father, Daughter believed to have lived. No details known. No further information. File closed.]

Dated: 12 April 2017.

Richard felt a lump in his throat as he read the stark facts.

"So," he thought, "mother pregnant at eighteen, stayed looking after the child until he was sixteen, moved to the metropolis, became pregnant again and died aged thirty six. What a sad little life and what a desperate start for the young boy. Despite all that, he seemed to have shined until he seemed to have thrown it all away and ended up in France."

From the limited chat he had had with Smithson it appeared that John Vince had been a highly rated officer and quietly recommended to '5' while working for the Tactical Unit and for some unknown and unrelated reasons had decided to abandon what would have been a highly promising career for a life (as Smithson sniffily put it) "being a beach bum in the South of France flogging second-rate paintings." The Office had, however, stayed in touch and used Vince "as and when necessary and of value." He had apparently established some useful contacts but refused to disclose them.

Richard knew in his heart that he should try and find these contacts in Biot, but perversely decided that Mougins sounded the most attractive place.

He would go there tomorrow.

CHAPTER SIX

Dr Peter Jordan, MB, BS, MRCGP smiled at his daughter and reflected how blessed he was with her, with his new surroundings and indeed with everything.

"Sian, you know I would be totally delighted if you moved into this neck of the woods. I think though that we have to set out our joint ideas on rules of engagement. For example I would not want you to live with me here, in this house, and I suspect that you would understand and agree with that. I have my own life to lead and you, yours. We will not always agree, you and I, nor should we. We are both grown up and reasonably intelligent people. There will be times when we need each other and times when we certainly do not. Agree?"

"Dad, you really are a pompous old fart sometimes but yes of course I agree. I really do not see it will be a problem."

"Rule one, Sian, Do not ever, ever again call me an old fart. Even," he went on reflectively "when I am."

"Yes, Dad, sorry."

"Rule two, young lady, is not to say sorry all the time. Anyway half the time you won't be sorry, will you?"

"No. Probably not," and she smiled in the way that could melt his heart every-time.

"In the meantime," he said gruffly, "look for a place to rent. Don't buy at this stage. We need to know whether it will work or not!"

"Oh, it will work!" she said confidently. "I've been thinking about you, this village and life here. How long have you known Richard Merrington, for example?"

"Probably six months or so, I suppose," he said, "why do you ask?"

"Do you think he is a man with a past and a secret?"

"Yes to the first; probably to the second, I suppose. What odd questions. You don't fancy him do you?"

"What's not to like?" she said with spirit, "A good looking man of mature years, single, I assume, with a past and some dark secrets; what's not to like?"

"The fact that he is at least twenty years older than you?"

"Which shows how little you know about women, Dad! But anyway that's not why I asked. Do you remember him asking about that headstone behind the church?"

"Yes, of course. I suggested he talked to Tom at the pub. Why?"

"I'm just curious. I went to see the headstone for myself the other day. It is rather odd. I think I'll talk to Tom and find out if he has discovered anything."

"Well I don't suppose Richard had any chance to talk to Tom before he went away on the very sudden holiday of his. Now that was odd; one minute he was here and the next off to the South of France. None as curious as folk," he contemplated with a sigh. "So, yes go and see Tom if you like. Is he also one of your paramours?"

"You never know," said Sian, coquettishly, "you never know!"

*   *   *

"Not much to report!" said Tom, as he tidied the chairs in the bar area. "Met a young lad called Stefan Williams who has joined XL Solutions, just up the road, and he was going to see if it had anything to do with them. Haven't heard yet, but it is early days."

"Mmm," Sian mused, "but surely the church will have some records. You can't just go along to a churchyard, plant a body and erect a headstone without permission can you?"

"Wouldn't have thought so," said Tom, "but maybe the problem is we haven't had a proper vicar for as long as I can remember."

Sian looked up sharply at Tom.

"Say that again Tom, why haven't you had a proper vicar, as you call it?"

"Because the church can't afford it I suppose. We have a parish vicar who looks after about seven churches in the area as well as us. We see him, or is it a her, I can't really remember, on high days and holidays, as you would say."

"Probably on religious festival days," corrected Sian, "So not as frequently as he should, do you think?"

"Well, we are a long way from the next village," Tom replied, "and I doubt the congregation ever exceeds fifty, except at Christmas, so it is not surprising, I suppose."

"But, don't you see," said Sian excitedly, "that's it! That's exactly what happened. Somebody buried Freddy Carol without any permission and then could not resist putting up a headstone."

"And no-one noticed?" Tom challenged, "after all these years?"

"It is not as unbelievable as it sounds," reasoned Sian. "Particularly if the parish vicar was replaced from time to time. Everyone imagines it was all above board – obviously permission had been granted in the past, they all think … but what if it never had been? In any case it is an out of the way spot and only seen by a few – by Richard and me most recently, but from all accounts not many others."

"Well I'll be damned," said Tom slowly. "Well I'll be damned" he repeated.

"Almost certainly, Tom," said Sian cheerily.

At which point, as if he was an actor performing his part, exactly on cue, Stefan Williams walked into the pub.

Tom introduced Stefan to Sian and, formalities over, questioned him about the mysterious headstone. Stefan was a shy, withdrawn man in his early twenties and was uncertain how to proceed. Tom sensed he would have been more forthcoming had Sian not been there, although he did seem to relax a bit in their company and sipped a non-alcoholic beer as he spoke.

"I had not appreciated how many people worked at XL Solutions." he explained, "The few I have met seemed pleasant enough, although I think most of them have only been there a couple of years or so. I was able to have a few words with the wages clerk, mainly to sort out a few gaps in my records. He has no record of anyone with the name Carol on the payroll in 1994 but that doesn't mean much, in my view. I think he struggles to keep the current records up to date let along being able to find information going back twenty years."

"He was all right about it, was he?" Tom was beginning to feel he might have started more than he bargained for.

"Oh, I think so. He seemed a bit on edge, but he probably thought I was the Chairman's son surreptitiously checking up on the workforce! No, he's O.K. and I am the new boy don't forget, so I need to keep my nose clean. So, if you don't mind I will duck out of your little enquiry from now on!"

Sian laughed. "Of course. It is just a silly mystery that's all! As you will find out, it doesn't take much in the way of gossip to intrigue the village folk round here. Thanks anyway for your help."

*   *   *

"Not sure that took us much further," said Tom, "Freddie Carol was not apparently on XL's payroll and no-one seems to have any idea who he might have been!"

"Oh, come on Tom, Just because he was not an employee of XL doesn't mean much, one way or the other. Anyway what makes us think he was involved with XL? We latched on to that because they are in the area and employ lots of people who would be unknown in the village."

"I know that," said Tom, "but equally no-one in the village seems to have known him. I've asked around and I haven't even come across anyone who knows about the headstone!"

"Probably because not many church-goers visit the pub on a regular basis," Sian reasoned, "but I'm not sure yet that there is no connection, Tom. Did you hear Stefan saying the wages clerk seemed very jumpy; even nervous? I didn't read anything into that at all. After all if an employee who has only been there a few weeks starts asking questions about a name on the payroll list, wouldn't you be nervous, or even suspicious?"

"Maybe, I suppose it is a bit odd that the clerk didn't establish with Stefan why he was asking. Let's leave it at that for now and talk to Richard when he returns. He was the one stirring the pot, when all's said and done."

CHAPTER SEVEN

He knew it would be fiendishly expensive but Richard had insufficient confidence in either his own driving ability or that of the local populace to consider renting a car to drive to Mougins. The hotel did its best to arrange a taxi for what they called 'un prix raisonable', although his idea of reasonable was not the same as their's.

He asked to be dropped off in the village square by the war memorial, which he recalled from the papers supplied by the Office was next to the bistrot where Vince had had his last fateful meal.

He was deliberately early, intending to catch the bistrot before the arrival of lunch-time customers. Apart from two French-men arguing in one corner of the terrasse the place was practically empty. Inside a waiter was preparing tables where, pleasingly, it was both quiet and cool.

"Demi-pression s'il vous plaît," he ordered and when the beer arrive he thanked the waiter and tried to engage him in conversation. The waiter willingly pulled up a chair and sat at Richard's table, which he was not expecting, and which temporarily threw him off balance. It became clear that the waiter was only too glad for the interruption and proudly claimed that they should talk in English, "as my English, as you say, is extraordinaire." It wasn't, but Richard gladly accepted this unexpected bonus, particularly when Henri (for that was his name, he assured the Englishman) revealed that he was indeed the very waiter who had served John Vince on the night of his death.

"Are you les flics?" asked Henri abruptly.

"The police? No, of course not. Do I sound like one?"

"Who can say these days?" Henri replied ambiguously. "So you are la presse perhaps?"

"No, no, nothing like that. Let's just say I was indirectly related to the dead man."

"Ah, so you knew him well, then?"

"No, I had never met him. I knew his family very well and I promised to find out what I could to clear up the mystery of his death. The English police know I am here", which was as close to the truth as he dare go.

"Excusez–moi, Monsieur, but the patron needs to see me. I will be back shortly."

With this the waiter moved abruptly to the back of the restaurant and Richard could see him talking earnestly with the owner who then disappeared back to his office.

Richard waited patiently for some five minutes before Henri eventually returned, his friendliness suddenly dissipated. "I am sorry, Monsieur, but I have work to do and must prepare the tables. Would you please leave now?"

His attitude brooked no argument so Richard thanked him for his time and left the still empty bistrot.

The two gendarmes approached him as he left the café and suggested he accompanied them to the police car, discreetly parked in a side turning.

They spoke entirely in French, making no attempt to assist him as she struggled to understand everything they said. It was obviously a deliberate ploy; he could not believe that police in a tourist spot had no knowledge of English and indeed, they seemed to understand everything he said.

It became clear that the bistrot patron had tipped them off. These were "police municipale" under direct authority of the Mayor and Richard knew they only had limited powers to investigate.

Nonetheless he spent an uncomfortable twenty minutes in their company, as he repeated the story he had told the waiter. It was only when he emphasised that his presence in Mougins was with the knowledge of the British police that they reluctantly let him go. They had done what they came to do – to point out that he was on their radar and would remain there – at least for the present.

*   *   *

From MI5's limited report Richard knew where the shot had been fired and that Vince's holiday home was at the bottom of the lane. At the top in the main square was the "Agence Immobilière" which, unknown to Richard, had caught Vince's eye on his way home that fateful night. It was a long shot but Richard had nothing to lose.

"I am looking for any homes or apartments that you might have available for a week or so," he explained to the obse-quious young man who greeted him when he pushed open the door, "preferably in the vicinity of the main square, as I cannot walk very far these days," he lied.

Unlike the gendarmerie the salesman was eager to please.

"Bien sûr, Monsieur, but this is a very busy time of year. Les grandes vacances you understand. At what price had you in mind?"

"Cela importe peu. More important is the location."

"It is perhaps a tragedy that Monsieur has some difficulty walking. Par hazard, one of our best properties has unexpectedly come back on to the market. It is only a matter of metres from here but it is, I regret, at the bottom of a hill."

Richards interest quickened and he made an effort to sound casual and that "it might, still, be of interest."

"Is it worth me looking at it? Just in case?"

"Of course, Monsieur, mon plaisir. It is in the small lane next to this office. The house is empty at the moment and I can show you around now, if you like."

"Thank you" said Richard scarcely believing his luck.

Through the heavy oak door that formed the entrance, the view, to use estate agents' terms was "stunning". Set into the rock which formed part of the hill on which Mougins was founded, the front of the double storied house had uninterrupted views of the rolling countryside which eventually led down to Cannes some 15 kilo-metres to the south.

On a sunny May day the air shimmered in the heat and he could well understand the attraction the place offered to all its residents.

To his right a full size pool bubbled its filtered water while the automatic cleaner silently swept along the floor' keeping it immaculate.

"I'm surprised the owner doesn't want to stay here all the time!" he observed to the agent who had become a little less obsequious and was proving to be reasonably chatty.

"The owner is a registered company, Monsieur. If you want to stay here I must 'phone to get the owners' permission. normalement they telephone me and and tell me who is staying here next and when; in fact," he said, suddenly nervous, "that is always the procedure. Perhaps I should not even be showing you around. Please, have you seen what you need? Can we go now?"

"Yes, of course, but don't worry about it. I have decided it is not what I am looking for. Out of interest though I see there is a basement room, full of books and maps – I saw them through the window. Is that part of the letting?"

"No, no, not at all." Now the anxiety of the agent could not be hidden. "That is the owners' own property and is always locked and alarmed. Only the owners have the key. Now, please, I must insist we leave straightaway. You are no longer interested are you?"

"No, thank you, I am not. So you won't have to telephone the owner will you?"

"No, no thank you. I am sorry, I should not have brought you here!"

"No harm done," said Richard with a disarming smile, "I will even forget I have been here."

"Mille mercis, monsieur. Je suis oblige"

"Ce n'est rien."

* * *

He sat in the back of the taxi taking him to his hotel in Nice and thought long and hard about his fleeting visit to Mougins.

Apart from establishing that Vince had spoken in perfect French the waiter had been of little help. He had not heard the shot and indeed only knew what had happened after the police visited the bistrot the next morning and questioned him "du ton aggressif". Vince himself had apparently been of few words and pre-occupied.

It was, the waiter thought, about half-past nine and already dark when he left. He had eaten a steak frites with a glass of Provence red.

"He had left no tip," said Henri. as if this was the most important fact of the whole evening.

Richard's mind turned to Vince's holiday home at the foot of the lane. What was both curious and astonishing was that the estate agent had not even mentioned the shooting although clearly the gendarmes had been all over the place like a rash and that the victim was in effect, a client of the Agency.

Then there was something else about the house which bothered him but he could not pin it down. The place was neat and tidy to a fault, possibly the result of the police visit, although in Richards limited experience police were not that good at tidying up after a search. Then there were the basement rooms to consider. There was no sign of a forced entry by the genadarmes of anyone else come to that, so what they contained was a mystery. No, it was not that, thought Richard. It was the tidiness, the lack of any 'atmosphere' which somehow bothered him. If it was a holiday home surely there would be signs of past occupation,, of relaxation, of enjoyment, but there was none of that. Or was he just guilty of a febrile imagination?

They were approaching the outskirts of Nice when it suddenly struck him. In the course of one of two of his past excursions for the Office he had been shown a similar functional, austere and characterless building.

It had been a safe house.

CHAPTER EIGHT

"Welcome back, Richard," said Peter, as he poured his visitor a stiff scotch and soda at a cheerfully outrageous hour of the afternoon. "Good holiday, I take it, even if a little rushed?"

"So, so," smiled Richard, "it's always difficult to keep all the women in my life happy all the time."

"Quite so; I know the problem. From which I gather that you're not about to tell me why you suddenly dashed off, without a by-your-leave, even to your friends?"

"Absolutely correct, Peter. Anyway it's all totally boring. Meanwhile, what dramatic news from the heart of Hampshire?"

"Normal stuff. The postmistress was abused and her life-savings stolen, and the heron has eaten all the fish in the village pond and the vicar was caught in bed with a choir-boy."

"We haven't got a vicar, or a postmistress, come to that," Richard pointed out.

"Ah well, nor have we, but I'm sure the rest is true, or at least nearly. Talk of the vicar, or rather the lack of one, does remind me, though, that Sian may have some news for you about the mysterious headstone you were interested in."

"I'd almost forgotten about that. What's it got to do with Sian?"

"Don't ask me," Peter replied. "All I know is that Tom and Sian seem like Hercules Poirot and Agatha Christie these days. Taken over where you left off, it seems. All very MI5. They're all down at the pub at this moment, I think. Go and have a word with them."

"I will do just that," smiled Richard.

"And Richard, don't drive. You've already had a drink."

"Peter, the pub is five hundred yards from here. Even I can walk that far."

"Just saying," said Peter, sniffily.

*　　*　　*

Tom thought Sian was the prettiest woman he had ever seen. Not that he could claim to be any sort of expert on women; as the only son of farmer Hicks and his wife Muriel, his early life had been confined to the field and the milking sheds of the family farm. He had realized they were poor – the private lane to the farm remained a succession of tractor ruts which filled with water in the winter and became treacherously hard in the summer, while those of the neighbours glistened with newly laid tarmac. He had been taught to milk the cows while the next door farm boasted shiny stainless steel milking machines and his farm always seemed last in the queue for the harvesting machines at the end of summer.

He went to the local village school and heard stories about up to date technological facilities in the big city of Winchester. He kissed some of the local girls behind the bike shed, because this was what all the boys did but he could not afford to take them to the cinema as they did.

His father had left home soon after he was born. His mother struggled to provide him with a happy, if very poor existence but gave up the unequal struggle, contracted pneumonia and died just after his sixteenth birthday.

He had no alternative but to mature quickly. He took on farm labouring work because he was good at it, and studied at night to catch up with his peers. He lost his virginity after a Young Farmers Union dance to a woman ten years older than he who had, she cheerfully confided to him "been around the block a few times."

He was articulate and intelligent enough but bided his time as he gained experience of the world around him. In due course he wanted to strike out on his own, in what direction at the moment he was unsure, but his time would come, he was sure of that.

All his perspectives were put into confusion the day that Sian had arrived in the village. He had never met her like before and the combination of disarmingly good looks with quiet charm and a vivacious personality won him over completely. Uncertain as to how to deal with his own emotions he did what he knew best which was to revert to the introverted, uncertain nature of his formative years. He knew that as a consequence he seemed at times to be gauche and lacking in confidence but he felt more secure than if he tried to be forthcoming and forthright.

Sian, for her part, saw in Tom qualities of honesty and innocence which were sadly lacking in the materialistic world with which she had become accustomed. He was an attractive man without the sophistication which hardened the exteriors of too many of her acquaintances. She liked him and was happy to treat him as an equal in their fantasy game of "Who was Freddy Carol?"

They were seated on the bar stools of the deserted pub mulling over various theories when Richard appeared. He was welcomed into their company as Sian explained why the mystery had deepened and why the absence of a resident vicar had led to their conclusions, however extreme.

Richard inwardly smiled at their enthusiasm and saw that if it was to be dampened it would need a gentle approach.

"I think you have both done remarkably well to have got this far," he said, "but the trouble is there are still too many unknowns at this stage. We still have no idea of the identity of the man and while it is an attractive proposition, surely you are not suggesting that nobody either saw or questioned the grave and its headstone over a twenty year period?"

"No, of course not," Tom surprised himself with the strength of his reply, "but what makes us think that the burial took place when Carol died? It could have been years later!"

"Now, there's a thought," Richard looked at Tom with new respect, "but why should anyone dig up a body from its resting place, wherever that might have been, only to re-bury it in the village churchyard? And what's more," said Richard, warming to the theme, "burying it in secret in a part of the churchyard seldom, if ever used and out of sight to all but the nosiest of us?" With this he grinned at Sian as if they had been caught in some school yard prank.

He is definitely attractive when he smiles, thought Sian – perhaps he doesn't smile enough. Out loud she said, "More and more intriguing, but I am sure there must be an answer somewhere."

"It seems to me that you have to find the answers to some specific questions before we can reach any conclusions," Richard suggested.

"You said that we have to find the answers; aren't you including yourself?"

"Maybe, but I think you should count me out for the time being. It looks as if I am going to be very busy in the next few weeks or so, but there is nothing to prevent you two digging a little deeper. Don't worry about the identity of Carol at the moment. Answer some of the obvious questions first and I think the rest will fall into place."

"I thought you were supposed to be retired, Richard." Sian sounded slightly plaintive as the thought of working closely in the future with Richard faded somewhat into the background.

"So did I, Sian, so did I, but the past never lets you go."

"What did you do in your business life?" Tom was anxious not to be excluded from the conversation.

"Oh, this and that, mainly to do with insurance which meant travelling quite a lot," Richard replied. "Not quite as boring as it sounds" he said which, he reflected, must be the understatement of the year. "It had its moments."

"I'm sure it did." Richard could sense a slight degree of sarcasm in Sian's voice which he chose to ignore.

"Why don't we see what some of the questions are that you should tackle at this early stage? Incidentally I don't think we should talk to the villagers more than absolutely necessary. Someone out there may be very sensitive to any suggestion that there is something nasty in the undergrowth. People are funny that way. Also if you don't mind me saying so there may be a time when we have to involve the church author-ities and perhaps the police; in a nutshell, tread carefully."

Tom nodded his immediate consent. Sian, still slightly put off by Richard's reluctance to be immediately involved, hesitated but then showed her agreement, recognising the sense of his remarks.

"O.K. Richard," Tom was determined to take a positive lead, "so what are the next steps to take, in your view?"

"Firstly, picking up on the very good point you made Tom; can we in some way or another find out when the burial did take place? I think asking around is out but there are probably other indicators to be found. Secondly have you explored the Register of Deaths or Burials for any record of Carol? You may have a problem here, because from what I know of Hampshire village records in many cases they have been lost or subsumed into the City Council files, or even lost or burnt; but probably worth a try.

Next; although it will be a balls-aching job – oops sorry Sian – it is probably worth combing through the Hampshire Chronicle starting when Carol first appeared on the scene right up to recent times to see whether there were any events worthy of reporting in or around this village that could shed a light on our mystery."

"I'll do that," Tom said without hesitation.

"It certainly seems enough to be getting on with," said Sian. "Sounds as if you are quite experienced at this sleuthing work, Richard."

"I used to play cops and robbers when I was five years old," he laughed, "and I never won, so don't hold out too many hopes!"

Sian looked at him quizzically. "And when might we be graced by your presence again my Lord?"

"Who knows?" retorted Richard "Maybe when Tom next offers me a free beer?"

"Or when you have settled up for the ones you've already had," replied Tom swiftly.

Tom was definitely growing up at a fast rate, thought Richard as he stepped out of the pub into the pouring rain.

CHAPTER NINE

He met Mr Smithson by the entrance to Winchester Cathedral, only to find that the two of them had been booked on the next official guided tour of the main building due to commence at noon. Inevitably Smithson was of drab appearance: indeed Richard would have been disappointed had he not been. It was Smithson's persona to a T.

"In a crowd is one of the most anonymous places to be," explained Smithson, "and on a guided tour there are plenty of opportunities to speak. I am surprised to see you back so soon. Any success?"

"You are the best to judge that." He summarised his visit to Mougins, spelling out facts not opinions.

"This holiday home, you said something about the place bothered you. In what way?"

"Oh, I don't know. It's just as if I had been there before, which of course I haven't. Just something about it. Reminded me of a safe house."

Smithson stopped abruptly, causing the American behind almost to collide into him and to depart muttering something to his companion about "These crazy English, I'll never understand them."

"What on earth would remind you of a safe house? Have you ever been in one?"

Richard nodded. "More than one. Pay no attention to me. It is not a fact, just a feeling. Does the Office even have safe houses overseas anyway?"

"No," Smithson was thoughtful, "but the 6 Office may have, I wouldn't know – leave it with me, I will come back to you. Anyway what about Vince's contacts in Biot? Have you been there yet?"

"No, I wanted to update you as soon as I could. I am hoping to go back next week."

"As long as you don't expect the Office to pay two return club class tickets to Nice." said Smithson and Richard could not decide whether he was joking or not.

*   *   *

He was not sure whether he liked Biot. Set on the edge of a long defunct volcano it could trace its history back to Roman times and parts of the Commune were un-deniably attractive in their old age.

Situated on a hill top only four kilometres away from the Mediterranean and with Antibes six kilometres to the south east it should perhaps have flourished but with only a handful of struggling hotels it attracted mainly day trippers and numerous holiday rentals. With a population of less than ten thousand it was never going to appeal to the affluent tourists who flocked to the Cote D'Azur.

Richard struggled with his French vocabulary and with some surly inhabitants before he found his way to Rue de l'Inconnu, which he thought was a highly appropriate address for an MI5 agent.

The street was in the old part of the town, tucked behind the Place des Arcades. It was narrow and damp, bounded by tall forbidding buildings with crumbling facades.

It was, he decided, not his first choice for a holiday address. It was forlornly empty of life, other than for a stray cat scavenging refuse from the gutters.

As he walked looking for the house numbers, he spotted an open doorway in which sat a dishevelled man whittling away at an anonymous piece of timber with a kitchen knife. Summing up his best French, Richard politely asked the man where he could find "Bâtiment numéro quartorze 'a', s'il vous plaît Monsieur."

To his astonishment the man grinned as he answered.

"Strewth mate, with an accent like that you have got to be a Pom!"

Despite himself Richard smiled, overlooking the slight on his linguistic talents.

"I really had not expected to come across an Aussie in the backstreets of a non-descript French commune," he said.

"There you are, then. Win some, lose some," said the man enigmatically, "see the world and pay your debts, that's how I look at it. Now, where was it you wanted?"

"Number 14(a). I said I would look up a relative of mine if I was ever in this neck of the woods. Not that I have ever met him but he is a mate of a mate, if you see what I mean. Sorry, I should have introduced myself. My name is Richard."

"Of course it is. And you can call me Oz; everyone round here does. What does this relative of yours do for a living? Assuming he does something that is; quite a lot around here don't bother."

"I'm told he was a bit of a painter – quite a good one. Watercolours and the like."

"A bit arty-farty then. I tell you where you could try. About two hundred metres from here you will come across a pair of wooden doors. Not quite sure about the street number but inside it's like a big barn and a lot of so-called artists hang out there. It is a good as place as any to try."

"Thanks Oz, sounds promising. I'll give it a go."

"You are very welcome. By the way Richard, does anyone ever call you Dick?"

*   *   *

He found the double doors which had no street number displayed so he was doubly grateful to Oz for pointing him in the right direction. Not only was there no street number there was neither door knocker nor letter box. Richard could only guess that the occupants never received any post, or that the postman pushed letters under the door. He had little choice but to hammer on the doors with his fist and as he did so he realised they were not locked. He pushed the right hand door which opened with a screech of hinges but there was no response when he called out. He edged his way into the barn, his eyes gradually adjusting to the gloomy interior. Underfoot was a bare concrete floor, partly covered by leaves and accumulated dirt left over many years by the boots of visitors The slightly foetid atmosphere offended his nostrils and the hairs on the back of his neck rose as he realised the perilous position into which he had had put himself.

From somewhere in the gloom a man said quietly "Qui est-ci?"

He turned to the direction of the voice.

"Désolé, mais la porte était ouverte. Je m'appelle Richard, Je suis anglais et je suis à la recherche d'informations"

"Un instant!" The man had by now found the light-switch and the barn came alive as the shadows mainly disappeared. Above his eye level Richard could see the man leaning against a balustrade; a stocky figure dressed in casual trousers with a loose fitting shirt or smock. He was bearded with tousled hair and his English was fluent.

"So, Monsieur Richard, my name is Jules. Why are you here and what makes you think anyone here can help?"

"I am trying to trace a distant relative of mine. I've never met him but I am told that he is a painter living somewhere in Rue de l'Inconnu. A man a few doors away thought he had seen a number of youngish men coming and going from here who could well have been either writers or artists."

"That will be Oz," said the man unpleasantly, "never could keep his nose out of other people's affairs. Wait, I am coming down."

He made his way down some rickety steps and Merrington saw his clothing was both torn and soiled. As he approached, Richard could smell both alcohol and an unwashed body and he wanted to blurt out an apology and run for the exit but he was determined to follow the only slight lead he had.

"We have many so called artists here," said the man, Jules, aggressively, "but I doubt if I know any of their names. So I think you will be wasting my time."

His English was faultless but his accent indicated some European influence. Not French, Richard thought, but possibly Caucasian.

"I do understand but perhaps you would hear me out," he said, as pleasantly as he could in the circumstances, "but I and some friends are anxious to find out where he is and if, indeed, he is still alive. We would, of course, expect to pay for any information that might help."

The man's attitude visibly softened.

"Just because I may not know his name does not mean that I cannot help. What would it be worth to you if I offered to ask around?"

"It all depends what you find out. I am only an agent for other people who, I imagine, have some financial interest in finding him. They asked me because he is a relative of mine and I can possibly find out more than by going through, shall we say, more official channels."

"In other words, the police. Rest assured, my friend, any contact we

45

have with the police is purely involuntary, if you see what I mean. Do understand, Monsieur Richard, that I am the only person who may be able to help you. I suggest that you tell me the name of this relative of yours."

"There is little point; you said yourself that you do not know the names of the artists that come here. What I will say is that my relative is English, but has lived in France for some time. He would be about forty and made a living selling water colours of this area to tourists, in the main. Can you recall seeing him here?"

"Maybe, maybe not. But if I do remember it will cost you. Comprenez?"

"Oh, I understand you perfectly," said Richard, "but as you haven't told me anything I can see little point unless you have some inform-ation, or you can remember seeing him. Perhaps I should now leave."

The man called Jules aggressively took a further step towards Richard who, calmly enough, said: "I suggest you now get out of my way."

Taking a further step forward, Jules grabbed the lapels of Richard's coat and put his face just inches away, breathing Pernod fumes as he snarled, "Now look here, cretin! You come in here uninvited with your schoolboy French and think you can get information as it suits you and that there is no price to pay? Laissez tomber, d'accord? If you cannot pay then there is no inform-ation. Understand?"

The man was drunk, probably on drugs and Richard knew he was playing a dangerous game but he had gone too far to back out now. He was convinced, that Jules knew far more than he let on. He just had to push a bit further.

"I only have two hundred euros with me but if you can persuade me that whatever you know or can find out is worth more then I will listen. Otherwise, forget it." he said defiantly, feeling less secure than his voice implied.

Then, suddenly: "Robert, Jean, Edouard. Venez ici." In response to the rasping command from Jules three shadowy figures emerged from the darker recesses of the barn like ghosts at Banquo's funeral. They stood, arms crossed, faces hidden in shadow in a semi circle some twenty yards behind Jules. If their intention was to frighten Richard, they had succeeded. They also blocked any chance of him making a quick get-away.

"Stay here" Jules moved over to the group of three men and engaged them in rapid French argot, virtually incompre-hensible to the English-man. One of the group kept watch on his every movement rendering escape virtually impossible.

Jules rejoined him after a few minutes, marginally less aggressive.

"It would seem one of my colleagues may have seen the man you are looking for but that was some time ago. I am prepared to let him talk to you if you pay the two hundred euros. Also I wish to be at the meeting as he does not speak English and your French is not good enough. I shall be the interpreter."

"How does that work out exactly?" Richard said, sardonically. "I pay you two hundred euros to let me talk to one of your gang, who may have information or may not. For all I know I may get anything or nothing. Hardly a fair deal. I don't think I'll bother."

Jules was furious and showed it.

"Listen to me, you stupid old man, either way you pay me the money. That is the price you pay for breaking into my building. Let us be clear about this: I own this property and the only laws that apply here are the ones I make. So you can forget about the police or the British Embassy. They cannot help you, my friend, you can only help yourself. Everyone who comes here, whoever they are, pays for the facilities I offer and in your case the charge is two hundred euros. Got it?"

As if on a signal the three man in the outer ring moved a little nearer, tightening the circle.

It would have been difficult for him not to "get it". He handed across the money from his wallet and Jules called across to the youngest of the group. Richard understood some of the French spoken by Edouard but it was far too rapid for him.

"He wants to know the name of your relative and whether he spoke good French?" In all the circumstances he could see little point in refusing to give this information for, as far as he realized, he was the only one who knew that the man was already dead and hardly likely

47

to be traced.

"John Vince, an Englishman but who also had a French passport, so I imagine he would be fairly fluent."

"Why do your friends want to contact him? Does he owe them money? Why did they ask you to help?"

"He is a relative on my wife's side. I know nothing about him but because I speak some French and know this area she asked me to help. I think his business partners need to find him, possibly to do with money, but I'm not sure. So, has your friend met him or not, and how can I make contact with him?"

"He says he frequently came here with a friend, but that was at least six months ago They were both interested in painting scenes of this area and for some time we provided easels and paintbrushes for a fee. He has not seen either of them since."

"And that's it? That's all I get for two hundred euros?"

"Of course, but Edouard says he should be able to find out much more if he talks to a number of his painter friends, but there will be a price."

"Now, there's a surprise." said Richard sarcastically, "You have just robbed me of all my euros and then you expect me to pay again? The only way you will ever see me again is if I have fool-proof guarantees that you have information that I need and that I will come to no harm."

"You have been seeing too much American television, my friend. There is little point in us harming you unless you do not keep your side of a bargain. We will keep ours – Edouard is to find out all there is to know about your 'relative'. Depending on the extent and value of that information you will to pay us an appropriate fee. It really is quite simple as I am sure you and I will agree on the size of that fee, won't we?" and Jules smiled, terrifyingly, at Richard.

"And in case you are still worried about your safety, I propose that we meet again, in three days' time, in the foyer of your hotel to conclude our little deal."

"You don't know where that is!" Richard protested.

"Of course I do. I saw the room card in your wallet when you kindly paid our fee. And do not worry, mon ami, I can scrub up surprisingly well if I have to. Shall we say twelve noon on Wednesday, then?"

With that he gestured to one of his trio to escort Monsieur Richard Merrington to the door of the barn and propel him into the sinister dusk of Rue de L'Inconnu.

CHAPTER TEN

"I don't know about you," said Tom, "but I am heartily sick of reading back issues of the Hampshire Chronicle and I should think the staff at their offices are heartily sick of me. The worst thing is I am not really sure what I am looking for. I've started at 1994 and searched for something startling that happened in the village and worked my way through fifty-two copies a year and have only just reached 1997! Nothing at all!"

Sian was sympathetic, the fun seemed to have gone from what started as an exciting treasure hunt.

"Do you know Sian, I am beginning to think that we live in the most boring place in the whole of the United Kingdom. It is true that babies are born and people die here but that does not strike me as unusual. I think I am beginning to lose the will to live. I assume there is no progress at your end?"

"Well, no but I have learnt some interesting facts but none of them seem to relate to Freddy Carol. Did you know for example that the Church owns the mineral rights in the land beneath virtually the whole village?"

"No, and I don't think I care that much!"

"You will do when they start fracking. I came across that little gem when I was researching what licences you need to bury someone. And what little I found out didn't help much. For example, before a funeral takes place in a licensed area you need a certificate from the Registrar of Birth and Deaths and to obtain a certificate you have to provide a death certificate from the GP (or hospital). So somewhere there is a record of Freddy's death – sounds like the City Council if there are no parish records available – but here is the interesting bit," Sian referred to her notes and quoted verbatim, "Burial ground managers may receive applications to re-bury remains which have been exhumed from other burial grounds." You don't need a fresh certificate from the Registrar but you have to provide documentary evidence which obviously includes the original death certificate."

"So your idea that Freddy's body may have been re-buried in the churchyard some years after his death while possible, seems a bit far fetched when you think of all the various permissions, licences and certificates that would have to be produced."

"Maybe," Tom admitted, "I really should have checked the Registry office before wasting my time reading back numbers of the paper. I will do that tomorrow. By the way, where is your Dad?"

"He was in the surgery, but he did say that he would be back for a quick lunch. Talking of such things, Tom, I thought you had a job to go to?"

"Have you seen the weather? I was supposed to be cutting back some of the hedges at the farm but what with the constant rain and a wind of 40 knots I was given the morning off. So I came to see you instead," he said, brightly.

Sian laughed. "Very considerate, I am honoured!"

"So you should be," said Tom, "think of all the other girls I could have chosen."

"In your dreams Tom, in your dreams."

The sound of the front door being opened bought an end to the mild flirtation and they shared a smile as the Doctor shrugged off his rain soaked coat and made his way to the kitchen where they were both sitting.

"Oh, hello Tom. Didn't know you were here – no farming today then?"

"Not in this weather, not this morning anyway." explained Tom "So I came round here to swap notes with Sian on where we have got to in our search. You know the mysterious headstone in the churchyard enquiry?"

"Ah yes," said Peter, "the secret enquiry which we can't talk about. At least not without Richard's agreement, I seem to remember. So how is it going?"

"It's not, really," said Sian, "it's all very frustrating. Tom should have seen the Registrar of Deaths by now but hasn't got round to it, have you my love?" and she smiled sweetly at Tom. She then quickly bought Peter up to date on progress, or lack of it, so far.

"The problem is, where do we go from here?" queried Sian. "Hopefully the Registrar may provide a clue."

51

"And I will be going there tomorrow." Tom said belligerently, now very well aware that this approach was long overdue.

"I thought you were going to see if there was any link to XL Solutions?" Peter queried.

"Dead end," replied Tom, "No record on their payrolls of any employees in the name of Carol. Not a usual surname that," he mused.

"Probably not that uncommon," said Peter, "I bet there are hundreds in the phone book – probably all born at Christmas" he said with a smile. "Well, best of luck you two; keep it up! At least I can tell the village gossips that all you two are doing this working on a joint project."

"Meaning?" demanded Sian.

"Meaning that you two are spending so much time together that tongues are starting to wag. Only joking," he said as he saw the expressions on their faces and in an attempt to move on said, "I do know the current boss of XL Solutions, but he only joined a few years ago so I doubt he will be able to help. His predecessor lives in the village you know – chap by the name of Oliver Brady?"

"He might be able to help; he would have been around in the 1990s wouldn't he?" Tom asked with growing interest.

"Sorry Tom, that would not work. First you promised Richard you would not ask around the village for fear of treading on people's toes!"

"Oh, yes," Tom's interest faded, "and the second reason?"

"You wouldn't get anywhere. I visited him yesterday and he is in the later stages of dementia. He has a full time South African carer who looks after him but I doubt that will be for much longer."

"Dad, are you in touch with Richard?" Sian tried to sound disinterested as she asked.

"Now and again, Sian. Now and again. I check his post and any calls on his answer phone. We e-mail each other when there is a need, why?"

"Just wondered. The headstone was his project and we are mere subcontractors! I do think it is time for him to express an interest and return from his holiday, or whatever!"

"I see. Well the last I heard was that he could still be some time. I am sure it is no holiday Sian, it's some business or another which is a legacy from his past; you know, before he retired here."

Peter knew enough about Richard's business to fend off questions like this; although not enough to even guess at what he might be doing.

He had a shrewd idea that he would not want to know.

* * *

"I've been waiting to hear from you all day," complained Sian. "Where have you been?"

"I told you I was going to the Registry Office today and that is where I have been." Tom was both tired and irritable and sounded it.

"What, all day?"

"Near enough. Now do you want to hear how I got on?"

"Of course I do; when did Freddy die?"

"I don't know. There is no record of his death in 1994 or three years either side come to that. It does not mean he didn't die in 1994 but if he did no one recorded it."

"Come on Tom, you must have missed it!"

"Sian, just listen to me. I have examined every entry in that sodding Register over a six year period. I have asked the Registrar herself for help. I have asked almost all the staff I could find until they threatened to throw me out. His death was not registered – got it?"

"Oh!" Sian expelled her pent up breath. "So now what?"

"Don't ask me, you're the educated one. Come up with some good ideas."

Sian sat back in the chair and thought. Thought about Richard, the church the headstone and finally Richard. They needed his leadership, his advice, his orders. He would know what to do. If only that man Oliver someone… Yes Oliver Brady. If only he was not so unwell living in the village with a full time carer.

"I have an idea," said Sian, "Someone must be able to help us; we don't need Richard." Secretly she knew this was not true.

Frustrated at the lack of progress so far, Sian admitted to herself that she had some good fortune when she was in the village shop looking to buy something to cook for her father's supper. She was acutely aware that staying under his roof was not ideal and the one thing that they had both agreed would not happen. Despite the efforts they had both made to find a suitable place for her to rent, or even somewhere to buy, they had continued to draw a blank. So she compensated by providing meals for them both, which meant a vast improvement for the doctor who, like most men living on their own, rarely bothered to improve on eggs or baked beans.

As she waited to pay behind a middle-aged woman, Sian could not help overhearing her conversation with the shop owner.

"I still find it unbelievable the price of avocados in this country. Where I come from you can buy a boxful for just a few cents!"

Her accent was not immediately apparent but Sian could recognise the clipping of the vowels and the cadence at the end of each sentence.

When her time came to be served she exchanged pleasantries with the kindly soul who worked so hard to scratch a living for herself out of the shop. As Sian collected her change she casually remarked she could not recall seeing the lady before in the village – had she recently arrived?

"Lord, bless you no, that's Mr Brady's carer, that is. She must have been here for some twelve months by now. That's longer than you have been here, I'm thinking. Poor soul, she does not get out much though what with Mr Brady being so unwell and all. Comes here regular, though, on a Wednesday afternoon, just to pick up provisions for the week. Nice lady; very educated I would guess with that South African accent of hers. Not much of a life though, I suppose. She keeps herself to herself, so to speak, but none the worse for that."

Sian made a note not to share too many confidences with the pleasant but garrulous shopkeeper. Her father would know the name of the carer.

It had been a straightforward matter to meet up with Mrs du Plessis at the village shop on the following Wednesday and within a short time, starting with shared consternation about the cost of everything, ending with a mutual exchange of first names; they agreed to a gossip over coffee the following Sunday.

"Normally I only have Wednesday afternoons off," said Helen du Plessis. "It is a legacy from the days when I had a maid. Maids in South

Africa, by custom, always had Wednesday afternoons off as their only break during the whole week. So when I had to look after myself I determined to follow a routine, having Wednesday afternoons off as strictly a time for leisure, but with the occasional Sunday as a special treat. Now that I am in the one in employment I have tried to carry through my routine as far as possible."

They met at a garden centre, a few miles away from the village where they could chat without being overheard. They had struck up an instant rapport. Sian genuinely enjoyed Helen's company and it made a welcome break from the predominantly male company in which she inevitably lived. Helen was immensely grateful to get away from the claustrophobic atmosphere of her job and the lonely existence where she was rarely able to communicate even with her employer.

"I did stay in South Africa for a while," Sian confessed over their second cup of coffee, "I was young and determined to travel the world. Johannesburg frightened me a bit but I loved Cape Town."

"I know what you mean" said Helen. "When I was young we lived just outside Johannesburg. On the face of it we lived a life of luxury – a maid, swimming pool endless braiis – barbeques to you – and plenty of friends, even if they were mainly Jannie's business colleagues. On the other hand at dinner, in particular, the talk was forever about the politics, the ANC and the violence. Our garden was surrounded by a six foot high fence and we employed a security firm to alarm the gates. To get to the bedrooms you went through yet another gate which you were supposed to lock behind you at night, but all that did was to increase the stress, You could not afford to be sensitive and in the end I adopted a hard shell exterior like most of the other wives."

"Did you have any family?"

"Children, you mean? No, Jannie was totally consumed by his work and was not interested in having children, nor, I have to say, in begetting them, if you see what I mean! Sorry, Sian, I did not mean to embarrass you!"

Sian smiled. "You haven't, don't worry. It sounds like a brittle life."

"Exactly," Helen agreed, "That's just what it was. I can see that now. It was only after my divorce that I started to see my existence for what it was."

"I am sorry Helen, I did not mean to pry." Sian felt a bit uncomfortable and wanted to steer the conversation into safer waters.

"You are not prying. I have no problems talking about my divorce. It was never going to work although in the early days we both tried; at least I think we did. Totally different backgrounds; Jannie was a rugby mad male Afrikaaner who could not accept that power had been given to the black South African. They are not a subtle race the Afrikaaners and their sense of humour – if they have one at all – is very basic."

"Not your sort of person, I would have thought," ventured Sian.

"No, but it took me a surprisingly long time to find out. Don't forget, you are only hearing my side of the story and I am probably still bitter. My background is of an English speaking family. Father was a Scot who emigrated to South Africa, found a job and married my mother when she was only eighteen. I had a good education which my parents could barely afford. Dad died when I was twenty-five and my mother a few years' later. I was young for my years and it just seemed to be the right thing to do. I needed security. Jannie was a good looking young man so I agreed to marry him; provided we spoke English at home and not Afrikaans. It was the only concession he made in our marriage. He slept around and I knew it, but it was not that unusual, and I forgave him at first until I caught him boasting about his latest conquest at a drinks party in our own home!"

"That's horrible!" said Sian quietly. "Thank you for telling me."

Helen laughed. "I bet you did not expect a warts-and-all story over coffee! I suppose I have been wanting to talk about it for a long time now – sorry it had to be you."

Sian moved on to more solid ground.

"So; how come you are over here? A carer in an English household?"

"I took myself to Cape Town with the limited amount of money I had managed to save, but that soon ran out and jobs were hard to come by. So I found a Care Agency and here I am!"

"Bit of a difference, I should think. How do you cope with our weather?"

Helen grinned, "Everybody asks me that! I knew what I was coming to and yes, of course I miss the sun but despite what you may think there is more to life than the weather!"

"You must be lonely though?"

"Yes, I am afraid that is true. It was all right when I first got here. Mr Brady was not too bad and only just diagnosed with dementia and was pleasant enough company. He would forget things and stumble over words from time to time but, particularly when telling me about his past he was both fluent and entertaining. He went downhill very quickly and now lives in a world of his own. I am just there to feed and wash him and to make sure that he does not fall too often. I am not grumbling; it was what I signed up for, but I am lonely these days. It can get me down now and again."

"It must do. There are a lot of lonely people in English villages, as I have found out. It's probably an age thing, with husbands often being the first to go, leaving the widows to struggle on their own. They are probably quite well off but have no appetite for establishing a social life on their own. I am sure I have no need to tell you but the English are in the main very reserved and many of them still live in a class-ridden bubble; although they would hate to admit it."

"So where do you fit into this class-ridden isolationist community?" Helen had a half smile on her face as she gently ribbed Helen.

Despite herself Sian coloured with embarrassment.

"Sorry that was a bit over the top, wasn't it?"

She admitted she had only newly arrived in the village and returned Helen's compliment by giving her a potted history of her life to date, omitting any reference to the headstone enquiry.

"So," she said, "does Mr Brady not have any children to look after him?"

"Oh, no. Well, in the circumstances, there wouldn't be, would there?"

"Sorry, what do you mean?"

"Of course, I was forgetting you have not been here long. I gather that at the time it caused quite a stir but these days it is just one of those things, isn't it?"

"I am afraid you have completely lost me!" Sian admitted.

It was Helen's turn to show embarrassment.

"I only know because he told me." she explained, "he never married because he was never attracted to the opposite sex, if you see what I mean," she finished, lamely.

Sian said, slowly, "You mean he is gay?"

"Well yes, although he didn't use that word I am sure that is what he implied. Didn't matter to me, of course, as it meant there was one less thing to worry about it."

"Yes, it would, I suppose. Still, it must have stirred a few feathers in the village."

"Maybe, but when he was running that local company…"

"XL Solutions," Sian supplied.

"Yes, that one. Sometime in the 1970's, I think. At that time he was living in a house someway out of the village, so I don't think it was common knowledge. He told me it was only after he retired that he sold up and moved to where he is now. I think that was in the late 1990s."

"At least he will have had your company for the last few months of his life," observed Sian, "It sounds like a dreadfully lonely existence up until the time you arrived."

Helen's face softened

"He is a good man and he has not been on his own all the time, I gather, from what he told me. He had a young man living with him for a while but that must have been over twenty years ago now. I think it must have been quite serious but he never talked about it and I have no idea why they split up. He has had an interesting life and it is a shame it has to end like this. Anyway it means I will be going back to Cape Town soon until I get my next assignment!"

And she smiled at Sian, a rather soft and wistful smile.

CHAPTER ELEVEN

Richard was pleased to see that the hotel lobby was busy with new arrivals booking in and others queuing to settle their accounts. At least, he thought, even Jules and his gang would hardly attempt violence (or even kidnap, as his vivid imagination had convinced him that this was a possibility).

Jules and another man arrived as a nearby church clock struck the hour. Richard hardly recognised his previous tormentor for, as he had promised, he scrubbed up well and even his clothes were far from shabby. The other man was a total stranger to Richard; a modestly but respectably dressed man in jeans and a white open necked shirt.

"This is François, François this is Richard." Jules wasted little time on formalities. He turned to Richard. "François is a friend of ours and he knows your relative John Vince. He is happy to talk to you but, as you know, at a price. I will leave him to agree with you an appropriate fee for his information and he and I will settle up later. Now I will leave you together. His English is better than your French, but not as good as mine."

With that he turned on his heel and strode out of the hotel, leaving Richard open mouthed in astonishment.

The stranger was a well built man; in his early forties with a suntan; evidence of a life spent in the open. Clean shaven, his blue eyes fixed on Richard as he smiled a welcome .

"I hope my English is not too bad," he apologised, "but Jules has to be better than anyone else in everything he does. C'est la vie!"

"Perhaps," Richard felt very defensive at the turn of events, "but I did not expect him to bring someone along who is not one of his "bande", nor not stay to drive a hard bargain."

François looked puzzled at this. Richard added helpfully, "ne faire pas de châteaux."

"I think your French is better than Jules believes. It is necessary for you to understand that in his own way he is an honourable man. You may not like the way he lives his life but he trusts people and many people trust him, of which I am one.

I am aware of his conversation with you and that you are to pay a fee for the information I will give you about John Vince. I will negotiate that fee with you after we have talked."

"As you like." Richard shrugged. "It is, to say the least, an unusual arrangement. As long as you understand that I have only agreed to hear what you have to say."

"Bien sûr Richard; may I call you Richard? It makes life so much easier don't you think?," and he smiled with the easy confidence of a man used to charming his way through life.

Despite himself Richard found himself smiling in return.

"I take it, then, that you have known John Vince for some time? I thought he lived in Biot at Rue de l'Inconnu but it now seems he was just a casual visitor there."

François laughed. "John lives anywhere and everywhere. He has no home of his own as far as I knew. I think he used Rue de l'Inconnu as a poste restante, if you see what I mean. It is true that it was there that I first met him. I am a very modest painter and I had been told that artists go there to exchange ideas, to smoke cannabis and to talk freely amongst themselves. I came along and met John. As simple as that."

"When did you last see him?"

"About two months ago, I suppose. We used to meet up at Jules's place but I have been away on business and John seems to have given up going to Rue de l'Inconnu. You have probably seen him more recently than me!"

"I have never met him," Richard repeated what he had told Jules. "I am often here in France partly business and partly holiday. My wife is related to him and had not heard from him for a while. What with that and some of his business colleagues anxious to meet him, it was agreed I would try and make contact."

"What business is he in?" François asked.

"You mean apart from selling doubtful paintings? Goodness knows, a bit of this and a bit of that. Very much like his sleeping arrangements by the sound of it. I don't even know whether he is alive or dead!"

François looked at him with an uncomfortable intensity. "Why do you say that?"

"What, whether he is alive or dead? Figure of speech in a way, I suppose. But he does seem to have disappeared from view. What have you heard?"

"Only whispers and rumours. You know what I mean; we both live in that sort of world. He and I became very good friends and I would be sorry not to see him again. We had a lot in common, he and I. He could get very angry at the total erosion of moral standards in every day life; a view he and I shared, but he was far more passionate about the lack of leadership in the West and what we should do about it. We talked about that just before he went on his "soi-distant" holiday."

"Why 'so called'?" Richard was curious.

"You never quite knew with John," explained the French-man, "he could be a strange one. I mean to say, surely his whole life was a holiday? He had no-one special in his life and drifted from place to place. How on earth do you take a holiday from that?"

"I see what you mean," sympathised Richard, "where did he go for this 'so-called' holiday?"

"No idea. He seemed to have a lot on his mind recently and told me he was going away for a week or so "pour prendre des vacances". No more detail than that and with John you do not ask! I had hoped he would be back by now, though."

"Quite." said Richard. "You say 'he had a lot on his mind'; could you explain a little more? It would help."

"We often had long talks about many subjects which were 'philosofique'?"

"Same word," Richard said, "'philosophical', in English."

"C'est ça. But on this occasion he seemed agitated, as if in some way he was personally involved. I remember him saying it was not enough to criticize, we should all "se lever et être compté.""

"Stand up and be counted," mused Richard, "What do you think he meant by that?"

The Frenchman shrugged his shoulders.

"Who can tell? As I say, it was if he was telling himself to do something, rather than to criticise the world in general."

"Apart from the others who met up at Jules', do you know whether he had any sort of social life; did he have any friends that he talked about?"

François considered the question carefully.

"Difficult to say. I would think his social life consisted of a few drinks with whoever happened to be in the bar. I am almost certain there were no women in his life, as otherwise he would have mentioned it in the way than men do to each other. Come to think of it there was one man, a man called Ryan who John mentioned a few times. I would hardly call him a friend though; he had obviously upset John in some way. From what I can recall he was an American. That would not be why John disliked him, as he was not that sort of person, but he had met him a few times and commented how loose-tongued he was, which is exactly what John was not. He and I would talk about many things, but in a general sense, which is why I remember the man's name. It was unlike John to talk about any individuals in such a way."

"Do you know whether Ryan was a surname or Christian name?"

"No, I suppose being American it could be either," François replied. "We were talking as usual about the complete mess the world has got itself into and John was saying he had bumped into this chap called Ryan who reckoned he had the answers to it all. As if!" François smiled bleakly. "Anyway I remember him virtually exploding; 'Bloody Americans; they reckon they know it all. Don't they realise they are the problem?' So unlike John, but he immediately calmed down and refused to discuss it any further."

"Anything else you can remember?" urged Richard, "places, addresses anything at all?"

"No, if I had I would probably have tried to make contact. I remember him saying he had met Ryan in a bar in the old part of Nice but that does not really help, does it?"

"Not really," said Richard, "the best thing I can do, I think, is to look up some of his business contacts in England. There is not a lot of point in me hanging around here much longer. You are sure there is nothing else you can think of?"

"Not really. I can only repeat what I said earlier: John was very "distrait" when I last saw him and very out of character. I only hope that nothing has happened to him. He is, or was, a good friend. We must stay in touch, Richard. I do need to know one way or the other. I will try and remember anything else that may help."

His worried look was replaced by a broad smile.

"I promise I will not charge you if I do come across anything," he said, "that is, of course, provided we have settled on my fee. I have concluded that I have given you some leads that may help?"

Richard nodded in agreement.

"As I say, I will try to track down his business associates in England."

"I will therefore have saved you from wasting any more time here," François pointed out, "I calculate that I have saved you three days which, at the rate this hotel charges, means you have saved fifteen-hundred euros, so that is my fee. Agreed? Come, I will walk with you to the reception desk so you can obtain the money for me."

Richard could not help laughing out loud at the audacity of it all but secretly he did not think it seemed an unreasonable request.

The transaction completed, they shook hands before they parted.

"You must telephone me, Richard, with any news about John. I will give you my number. With that the Frenchman extracted a business card from his porte-feuille and handed it to the Englishman.

The card said simply "François. t: +33 (0) 4 93 62 32 59"

"François – that's all?"

"It is my name and that is all you need to know. Yours is Richard. That is all I need to know."

Then, as they were about to part company, the Frenchman added:-

"I think I may have remembered the name of the bar. John once mentioned a 'Bistrot Bonheur' or something like that, saying we should meet there one day, but we never did. Au revoir, mon ami."

And with that, he was gone.

*   *   *

"How are you getting on with the Merrington business?" Geoffrey was bored; his was a mentally stimulating job, with moments of intense excitement and even danger, but there were times when those moments had been passed to others and all he could do was await results. The "thrill of the chase", as he liked to think of it, was largely the domain of the younger generation who physically and mentally were more capable than he to tackle the demands of the field work and to operate at the frantic pace which the job demanded.

He knew that retirement beckoned; partly he was relieved by the thought, but on occasions such as these he had difficulty in admitting that age had depleted his mental resources and his physical strengths. For some unknown reason his mind recalled Cleopatra. "Age shall not wither her, nor custom stale." Then she was a bloody lucky young woman, he thought, in a moment of selfish depression.

"I asked how you were getting on with the Merrington business?" he said testily and more sharply than he had intended.

The younger man looked up from his computer screen.

"Sorry guv."

Neil sensed Geoffrey's mood, if not the reason.

"The answer is good, in parts. I have kept you up to date in our debriefings," he gently reminded the older man, "but I am wondering whether Merrington is totally up to it and have asked for a meeting early next week. I'll know more after that, if I could have a chat with you then?"

"Of course," said Geoffrey, immediately sorry for his bad show of temper. "I just don't want to stray too far on this one," he explained.

"Point taken" said Neil.

*   *   *

Smithson met Merrington when he arrived on the British Airways flight from Nice to Heathrow and showed him into a private room where Neil was already waiting. Smithson introduced Neil as 'my colleague' and Richard accepted that further identification would not be forthcoming.

He quickly summarised the limited progress he had made, ending with the meeting with François and his reference to "Bistrot Bonheur".

"Presumably you followed that up and visited the bistrot?" Smithson queried, fairly aggressively.

"No, for three reasons. One, I was running out of time by then. I had been away ten days and I was ostensibly only taking a short holiday. Two, you asked for an urgent meeting and three, I have been unable to trace this café or bistrot or whatever you call it. The telephone directory doesn't list it, the internet has no record of it and the hotel had not heard of it! And you wanted this meeting." said Richard with some spirit.

Smithson looked at Neil who just shrugged.

"I am wondering," said Smithson, "whether we should shut this one down. We have lost an agent, to be sure, and it would be nice to bring it to a close, but we're in danger of treading on other peoples toes, and is it all really worth it?"

It was not a question for Richard to answer and he realised that Smithson was looking for a reaction from his 'colleague'.

Neil said:

"I agree, to a point, but from the limited information Mr Merrington has obtained," (Richard inwardly squirmed at the 'limited'), "I think it is worth digging a little further, but with considerable care."

Smithson slowly nodded his agreement and Richard stopped holding his breath.

"But," Neil went on, "I think, Richard, that you should hold back for now. There is a risk in becoming too exposed and I feel another team member would come in very useful at this point, do you not agree?"

Richard sat quietly for a minute, quelling his anger, then: "If you consider that I cannot finish the job that you invited me to do in the first place; then that is your decision, of course. I must say, anyway, that I was never attracted by the pay grade."

Both the men had the grace to laugh at this and the tension eased to a degree.

"Please don't take it so personally, Mr Merrington," said Neil, "but the risk of over-exposure is a real one. We just want you to take a break and let us develop some of the lines of enquiry you have opened up. It will be of great benefit to us if we know that you will make yourself available to us, as I am fairly sure we will have a further need of your skills."

It was a speech from an arch-diplomat, as Richard knew well, but it did what was intended and restored some of his battered pride.

"You may be interested in a couple of aspects which you will not have had sufficient time to think about," Smithson interjected, "for example, we took on board your suspicion about the holiday home Vince had rented. You may remember that it reminded you very strongly of a safe house, which, as I said at the time, the Office does not generally operate in overseas territories. We have worked behind the scenes on this one but it has now become clear that it is a genuine holiday let. It might not be to everyone's taste, but it seems that it is run from a distance by a subsidiary of a German firm, with typically Teutonic rules and regulations which does not make the life of the French letting agent particularly easy. It is, however, all apparently legitimate and above board, so we can put that one to bed for now. Personally I wouldn't be surprised to find that there is a money-laundering angle somewhere down the line, but that's not our problem."

"I see," said Richard thoughtfully, "and the second point?"

"Ah," interrupted Neil, "it did occur to me that more time needs to be spent on identifying the bistrot. Could it be known, for example, by a different name; perhaps in another language? I'm no linguist but does 'Bistrot Bonheur' translate into English?"

"'Bistrot means 'café', or maybe 'bar'," Richard replied slowly. "'Bonheur' is more difficult. It could mean 'good fortune', or 'good luck', or even 'happiness'. I'll do a bit more research."

On the train going home he shouted "Yes, of course" and then had to apologise to all the other passengers in the first-class carriage. He grabbed his copy of The Evening Standard and wrote across the top:

"PUB BLISS"

He even knew where it was.

CHAPTER TWELVE

Peter Jordan listened intently, saying little other than the odd "I see," and at the end of the call, "Understood, you just make sure you look after yourself". He put the receiver down and stood immersed in thought.

"Are you all right, Dad?" Sian broke in, "was that one of your patients? You were on the 'phone so long I thought it must be a new girlfriend!"

The doctor shook his head slightly as if to clear his head and smiled at his daughter.

"No, not this time darling. If you must know that was Richard. He is back in the country."

"Oh, good – what news if any?"

"Nothing for you to bother about Sian. It is just that he has come back with a lot of business problems and he doesn't sound like his normal self. I must admit I am a little worried about him. He would not tell me what these problems are but he did ramble on about how he had let people down; how he was no longer to be trusted. He sounded very low."

"Anything you can do, Dad? Some sort of medical help, perhaps?"

"Hopefully we are not at that stage yet," said the doctor, "he is going to spend a few days with his daughter to get away from it all. I am sure he will be fine."

*   *   *

Jan Merrington lived in a small flat on the top floor of a non-descript one-hundred-year old building in an unfashionable part of the East End of London. Ever since her unpleasant divorce she had lived alone and happily so. Her job, ostensibly for the Ministry of Defence, meant she spent long hours at her desk with highly classified information unable to be shared even with close colleagues, and the flat proved to be a welcome oasis from the combination of tiredness and stress.

She rarely saw much of her father these days and this was by tacit mutual agreement. They spoke regularly enough and very occasionally spent time together but each had their own lives to lead, their own interests and their own needs.

Her father had pursued an eventful and rewarding business life and she suspected that this had been driven, in his later years, by a wish to sublimate some of the loneliness he undoubtedly suffered. He was a private person, honest and loyal to a fault and she could sense, as retirement loomed, that there would be gaps in his life which would need to be filled. She had little hesitation is mentioning his name to her immediate superiors at an appropriate moment and was gratified to learn he had been of value to her employers from time to time without being told either by him or by them the nature of these assignments.

She was at all times comfortable in her father's company; he had both warmth and humour in his make-up which surfaced when he was relaxed and with people he could trust. His loneliness had bothered her for a while but it was not for her to interfere and it was not a subject ever raised between them.

She had therefore been shocked by the meeting, some months previously, with two of her superiors who had come to the difficult decision that she should be told that her father was not well. A form of mental stress they said, following an assignment abroad that had not gone according to plan. It was important that she knew enough to understand that for a time he might be difficult to approach and to be resistant to any well meaning words from her. They were certain that he would not tell her about the project and nor should she ask. It was only because of her position in the Office that they were able to pre-warn her. They felt that she should know that on this particular assignment he had worked closely along-side a woman who had died in "difficult circum-stances" and her father had been traumatised, unfairly blaming himself for her death.

She had not heard from him for three months after that but then one day he called her and it was as if nothing had happened. The subject was never discussed and they renewed their relationship without any obvious embarrassment on either side. And now this latest phone call.

Jan had readily agreed to her father's request to stay for a few days, as she enjoyed his company, but the stress she could hear in his voice reminded her too vividly of that dreadful time in the past when he had buckled under the strain.

*   *   *

As she knew they would, they both seemed to pick up where they had left their relationship when they had spent two days together the previous Christmas. They were relaxed in each other's company, although her father was quieter than normal; more introspective.

Many years before they had discovered a Chinese restaurant by the Thames near Wapping, which they both declared to be a favourite, with impeccable food and superb family service. It became a tradition that they dined there on the first evening of each visit Richard made to his daughter.

The tables were a discreet distance from each other allowing private conversations without fear of being over-heard. The owner, beaming with delight, showed them to a table in the corner of the restaurant and personally delivered a bottle of chilled Pouilly Fume as he had done many times over the years.

"Michael never forgets, does he?" said Richard, once they were on their own. "I wonder if he realises by now that we never actually finish the bottle?"

"Though I think we get close to managing it every time we come here!" laughed Jan.

"Ah well, who is counting?" smiled Richard, "although I think one bottle will remain our maximum at those prices!"

"So, Dad how are you? Really, I mean? It is lovely to see you but I have seen you looking better and you seemed slightly stressed on the 'phone."

"Jan, I have no wish to spoil these few days with you but I had to get away from it all and I could not think of nicer company! So thank you for putting up with me and I promise to lighten up!"

"It seems to me," said Jan, "that you should tell me as much as you can, or as much as you want to, so that we can both park the problem on one side and enjoy each other's company as we have always done in the past. Agreed?"

He smiled at her and his face softened, It was if the clouds had already started to clear.

"You are too old for your years sometimes, young lady," he said, "Of course I agree; if you are happy for me to let my hair down for a few minutes then yes, that's exactly what we will do. As you know only too well. I have been able to help the Office out from time to time over the years. Bits here and there; nothing too dramatic, nothing too involved and I have been both pleased and privileged. I think it worked."

Jan nodded. She did not want to interrupt him and was happy just to listen.

"I had decided to retire fully. I was becoming bored and cynical with my own job and whilst the various "interludes" meant excitement and interest, I knew I was only involved on the fringes. I had played my part and was happy to move on. So the last thing I expected was to receive another approach; this time requiring more commitment. They say there is no fool like an old fool and I jumped at the chance. That was my first mistake. Not that I regretted my decision, far from it. The problem was I made progress; I had broken down barriers and I wanted to go to the next stage. I genuinely believed I could find all the answers, or at least enough of them to count."

"And what was your second mistake?" asked Jan.

"Realizing that my belief was not shared by others," he said, "and I could not understand why not."

"Since when did you become an egotist?" asked Jan.

He smiled at her, accepting the criticism.

"Jan, Oscar Wilde once said 'I am the only person in the world that I would like to know thoroughly.' I, in contrast can't think of anyone I dislike more."

"Therein, I suggest is the problem. Come on, Dad, that is a silly thing to say. Tell me a little more about the circumstances."

"I am not sure I can tell you a lot more, if you know what I mean."

"Dad, lets stop pussy-footing around. You and I, in our ways, both work or have worked for the Office. Now, I remember when I started asking how much and how little I could say about what I did and I got a very commonsense answer. 'Obviously you must be careful about what you say and to whom you say it. Family is a possible exception, but even then be very circumspect.' As they said to me at the time 'We engaged you because we have complete trust in you, but at the end of the day it is you that is at risk and if you are careless you will be exposed; it will be you who has most to lose.' It is up to you, Dad, but I would have thought there was a fair amount of trust between us, wouldn't you?"

"Of course there is." He paused, digesting what she had said. "But I won't tell you so much that you could be compromised, if that is all right with you?"

"Agreed."

So he filled her in on the detail of the assignment without naming names that could be traced or specific places and made her laugh when he told her of his first encounter with Jules.

"You really have read too much James Bond," she said, "Our lives are much more mundane that that!"

"Maybe," he responded, "I must admit I started to wonder what I had got myself into. Anyway by accident or design I discovered the name of the place where our agent had met the American. It seemed to me my next move would to find the bar and to find someone who remembered our agent there with the American."

"Then what?" Jan questioned.

"Well, at least we might then have enough to identify who the other man was. Someone killed our agent in cold blood, that we know; what we don't know is why and when we have found that out we will know who."

Jan sat quietly for a minute, toying with her glass of wine.

"Dad, we both agreed we would talk about what is bothering you and after that we would put it to one side and get on with enjoying the next few days. So, at the risk of being Marjorie Proops, I am going to analyse what you have told me; give you my views and yes, if necessary give you some advice. I have been wanting to do that for years – advising my own father after years of him lecturing me!" She peeled with laughter at the thought.

"Very funny," her father said, a touch grumpily, "and how the hell do you know about Marjorie Proops? She was an agony aunt before you were even born!"

"Dad, when I was at boarding school we used to read all the rubbish newspapers, including the Daily Mirror. I can certainly remember Marjorie Proops! One girl in our class would send the most outrageous letters to her, hoping that she would take it seriously and publish a reply! Anyway to cut to the chase as they say...

"Firstly, your pride has been hurt by taking you off the assignment so soon, I am not going to say 'Get over it' as it is some little problem. To you it is not. I suspect your self confidence took an almighty knock when you were so badly hurt on that previous assignment and when the girl died, but we are not going there, Dad. I only mention it because things like that have a permanent effect and you will carry any hidden scars probably for the rest of your life. What to other people is a trifling matter of little consequence is not to you, and I respect that.

But look at it from the point of view of '5'. Your French is very good by normal standards but you are not and never will be fluent. That's not a criticism; it is just a statement of fact. So if you visit this bar and start asking questions you will stick out like a sore thumb. That on one side, you have already made yourself known to some very "iffy" people. You have put a wooden spoon into the murky depths of what sounds like part of the underworld and given it a good stir. You may have got lucky and may have got away with it; you may not. If you keep on stirring then you really are asking for trouble and the Office can see that. They are not fools, Dad. They are consummate professionals and they are pulling you away before you get into real trouble. As I see it the problem is that you are taking this as a personal insult, when it is no more than is necessary for your own protection."

Jan wondered, in the silence that followed, if she had gone too far.

"I am afraid," said Richard slowly, "I am afraid that you are right and I am being a bit pathetic aren't I?"

"No, Dad you are not; by normal standards it would seem that you have over-reacted but to anyone who knew about your previous disaster then it is totally understandable. If they said that they may want to bring you back in at a later stage then they meant it! Let the dust settle, Dad, and see what happens next. Go and enjoy your village life and settle some Parish Council dispute or other, if it makes you feel better."

Her father laughed with genuine humour.

"If only you knew, Jan; if only you knew! Meanwhile, shall we break the course record and order another bottle of wine?"

CHAPTER THIRTEEN

Peter had already added "Merrington" to his list of forth-coming home visits as he considered Richard to be someone he would like to get to know more, having only met him a matter of months ago. As a semi-retired doctor, village life had many advantages and few downsides but Peter missed having social contacts. The nature of his work was such that while his patients readily confided in him he had nobody he could turn to for help or guidance. He had a warm relationship with his daughter but, as was the case with his generation, this did not extend to sharing his inner fears or concerns with her. He instinctively felt that he and Richard had much in common and looked forward to developing their relation-ship.

It was therefore not by total chance that he found himself knocking on the door of the small but attractive thatched cottage at one end of the village. Richard arrived at the front door at the same time as his golden retriever who insisted being the first to greet the visitor by thrusting a wet nose into the welcoming hand.

"Sorry about that," said Richard, "he just loves people. Tom has been looking after him while I was away, so now Buster thinks he is entitled to nuzzle everyone to check they are not after his sheep."

"I think I follow that. Anyway he looks well enough, but how about you?"

"Oh, I'm fine now, Peter. Sorry if I alarmed you with my selfish drivel the other night. I must admit I was feeling a bit low at the time, but my daughter soon sorted me out with some well-directed home truths, as only one's nearest and dearest can. Fancy a drink? It is nearly six o'clock."

"You are the last on my list today so I must admit I am tempted. It's a bit early though isn't it?"

"Since when has temptation come at a convenient time?" said Richard. "The only decision is, which drink?"

They each settled on a glass of white wine while they sat on the patio and watched the sun cast longer and longer shadows.

"We make an interesting couple," said Peter, "both of us of an age and with both daughters of an age. Least, so it would seem to me. Maybe I am being presumptuous; I am approaching my sixty-second birthday and Sian is just about the right side of thirty, I think. I hope I've got that right; I will be in all sorts of trouble if not!"

Richard smiled. "Let me assure you, Peter, you both seem younger than that. I suppose that comes from having a doctor in the family! As for us; well I am fifty-seven and Jan is thirty-three. And as I, for one, look old for my years the comparison bears scrutiny!"

"Both single men contemplating their twilight years then," Peter's eyes twinkled as he spoke. "That is, I am assuming that you are on your own; like me. My wife died many years ago at a ridiculously young age."

"I am sorry to hear that," said Richard, "I was divorced about five yours ago – and please don't say sorry!" He said quickly, "I am sure it was all my fault, or so I was told at the time, so it must be right."

"Hmm," said Peter, "Well having got rid of those skeletons from the cupboards let's move on to happier things. Without giving any details, I take it your excursion to the south of France was not all holiday and wasn't totally enjoyable?"

"No and no! Thank you, by the way, for deflecting enquiries about my whereabouts; maybe one day I will be able to fill you in with the gaps."

"There's is no need, you know that. Here at home the mystery of the churchyard headstone continues to enthral. That is, it continues to enthral Tom and Sian, and I occasion-ally get scraps from their table. They will be glad to see their leader back and so will I, come to that. They definitely need you to take control otherwise there is a real risk they will end up libelling some poor villager!"

"As bad as that?" Richard exclaimed.

"Not quite, but close; you'll see"

So they finished off the bottle of wine between them.

*　　*　　*

Sian realized that her mother's legacy would go so far and no further and that she really had to seek some form of gainful employment. Her father had refused any payment for the two months' lodging she had enjoyed and it was definitely time to move on or risk disrupting their relationship.

With the better weather the property market had picked up and she decided to rent a small one bed-roomed flat forming part of a large Victorian house which had seen better days. The flat was clean and pleasantly furnished and it suited her while she looked for a suitable job.

She was excited about the flat and told Tom all about it at the first opportunity. He was pleased for her, although he expressed doubts about the lack of accommodation.

"You will have nowhere to put up visitors when you have them," he said.

"Well, with only one bedroom I will have to pick who I have to stay very carefully indeed Tom, won't I?" and she smiled at his obvious embarrassment.

Tom, although theoretically only a part time barman had none the less taken it upon himself to freshen up the bar areas. In his spare time he had totally redecorated, changed the curtains, persuaded the brewery to supply not only beer mats but also framed prints for the walls which as he said "drags us all from the threshing machines of the 1930's to the combined harvesters of the 1980's."

Sian sat on one of the bar stools and watched Tom polishing glasses. She had given up worrying about local gossip recognising that her regular visits to the pub would be interpreted either that she was a confirmed alcoholic needing a fix at six in the evening or that she and Tom were embarking on a torrid sex-fuelled affair. Neither had substance in fact and she was pleased at the first negative and unsure about the second. She had become fond of Tom with his kindness and courtesy and feared that to move onto the next stage of their relationship ran the risk of losing the warmth and security she treasured. Far from being un-attractive, it was his depth of character that appealed to Sian and yet she had no wish to disturb, let along destroy, that inner calm of his.

"Richard is back, at last" she said, deliberately interrupting her own dangerous chain of thought. "Dad saw him the other day and it seems he is home for a while now."

"Good," said Tom, "perhaps we can make some progress. Well, speak of the Devil!" as Richard walked into the bar.

"I know I am no Angel Gabriel but that's a bit unfriendly, Tom! All alone with sumptuous Sian I see!" and Richard blew a kiss to Sian, who felt herself colouring up as she smiled back.

"Goodness; you are in a good mood, or have you been sharing another bottle of Dad's wine?"

"No, no nothing like that. I am just glad to be back amongst friends. Talking of drink, though, I suppose a pint of beer would not go amiss!"

While Tom saw to the order, Sian was bubbling with the news of their discoveries.

"We decided not to go any further without talking to you," she explained, "but it does seem likely, doesn't it, that Oliver Brady's live in lover was 'our' Freddy?"

Richard laughed at her obvious enthusiasm.

"Now let's get this straight, Sian. Oliver Brady, the pre-vious MD of XL Solutions, employed a young man to be his companion sometime in the 1970's who apparently had disappeared from the scene by the time he moved house in the late 1990's. Your suggestion is that some-how Freddy Carol was buried in the churchyard with a headstone which says 1974-1994?"

"Exactly, but we don't see how we can take this further without talking to Oliver Brady."

Richard turned to the barman. "What's your view of all of this, Tom?"

"I think we are in dangerous territory," Tom counselled. "I was not very happy when Sian told me she had quizzed the South African carer. Somewhere along the line we are breaking into people's confidences, prying where we have no right to."

"Oh, thanks Tom for that vote of confidence! You seemed interested enough when I told you what I had found out!"

"Hang on you two," said Richard, "It's not going to help our cause if you end up squabbling with each other. You may have a point Tom and I pass no comment on the rights and wrongs of what Sian did, but my view is that we are where we are and there is not going back on it.

Agreed?"

Tom nodded. Sian said, "I suppose so," with a slight sulk in her voice.

"O.K." said Richard firmly. "First point, do we drop the whole thing at this stage? Why not let sleeping dogs lie? Are we risking upsetting people unnecessarily?"

"Surely we can't give up now, just as we are getting somewhere?" Sian was emphatic.

Tom said quietly "Aren't we forgetting something? We are talking about some young man who, it would seem, died at an early age in mysterious circumstances and no one gives a damn? At the least we owe it to his memory to keep going and establish the truth; obviously we must tread carefully and recognise sensitivities where they exist but I agree with Sian; we should not stop now."

"I was not suggesting that we should," Richard pointed out, "but I am suggesting that we carefully review the situation from time to time. Now let me go back to something you said Tom. You said Freddy died at a young age. What makes you say that?"

"The headstone 1974-1994. So he was only 20 years old."

"That depends on two things, Tom. One, yes if you believe what the headstone says. Two, what did Mrs du Plessis tell you, Sian? That Brady was running XL in the 1970s and employed Freddy, assuming for a moment it was him, at about that time. Let's say he was an adult at that time, perhaps eighteen to twenty. If he died in 1994, which the headstone implies, then he would be nearer forty."

Sian nodded her head. "Mrs du Plessis did not exactly say that but that's certainly the impression I got."

"Good point, Richard," said Tom. "always assuming Freddy was the same person that Oliver Brady took on as his lover."

"Quite," Richard agreed, "and we are a long way off proving that one way or the other. And here's another thought; if it was Freddy and he did work for Brady then 1974 would not, obviously, have been his birth date. So who is to say that the last date of 1994 was the date when he died?"

"Any chance of a drink on this place?" said a slightly peeved potential customer at the end of the bar.

"Meeting over," said Richard, "and it is my turn to buy the next round."

CHAPTER FOURTEEN

After his initial sulk, Merrington telephoned Neil on the private number he had been given. assuming that it was probably scrambled and therefore safe to talk.

Neil confirmed that Richard could tell him the name of the bar in Nice without mentioning that they had already worked out that Bistrot Bonheur was probably Pub Bliss, a reasonably well known watering hole in the old part of town. He nonetheless thanked him and promised to keep him in the picture as and when there were positive developments.

He was aware he was running solo on this and that Geoffrey, his immediate superior, only required regular de-briefings and had no wish to become involved beyond that. On the other hand Neil knew that there was a limit to his mandate and what he had in mind was probably above his pay grade.

He made his way to Geoffrey's office which he noted was not as plushly furnished as he would have imagined. Neither was his reception as cordial as it might have been due, no doubt, to Geoffrey's wish to distance himself as far as possible away from the enquiry.

Neil, nonetheless brought Geoffrey 'up to date' including the identification of Pub Bliss and the meeting between Vince and the American, Ryan.

"As I understand it from Merrington, Vince told François (we don't have his surname) that his discussion with Ryan became quite heated. If that is the case that it seems highly likely that someone at the Bistrot would have overheard it; maybe even the management." said Neil.

"But where is this getting us?" Geoffrey queried. "We seem to be a long way off discovering who shot Vince at Mougins. I cannot see where you are going on this, Neil."

"The row between Vince and Ryan, if that is what it was, is maybe an indication of ill-feeling which developed into an assassination. I know it is a long shot but for the moment that is all we have."

Geoffrey thought for a while, trying to take it all in.

"There comes a point Neil, when I have to consider whether it is worth carrying on with this investigation and I am not so sure that we haven't reached that point. I know that it is your show and that it must be your decision but I hope you take my comments on board. But if you still want to move on where do you propose going from here?"

"Don't worry Geoffrey, I have already had the same feelings when I briefed Smithson. It is all finely balanced, I agree, but I think it is worth one more push. What we need is for someone to talk to the manager of Pub Bliss and see if this spat between Vince and the Ryan individual was overheard at all and can in any way help us. If not, then I think we have reached the end of the road."

"So, why don't you just get on with it? It is your call Neil!"

"Because I may need some help on this one and I am not too proud to say so," said Neil. "I pulled Merrington off because his involvement was becoming a little too obvious and I have no wish for Smithson to be the front man. It needs someone who is part of the pub scene over there, probably French and able to move around without creating waves. I thought of François, the man Merrington met when he infiltrated the strange underworld gang but I know nothing about him; not even which side he is batting for. The deeper we go the un-easier I feel that we are moving around in '6' territory. I thought it might need some input from someone who could take an empirical view of it all, so here I am!"

"Old age does not imply wisdom Neil. I think I see your quandary but I think you are making too much of it. Leave it with me. I will give it some thought."

Neil knew Geoffrey would never be hurried.

*   *   *

He was at his workstation when Geoffrey wandered by and stopped for a chat.

"Sorted." he said, "Do come by my office when you have a free moment. It's not what you know, it's who you know," and off he wandered like a forgetful member of Lord's who had lost his way to the nearest bar.

"I just wish he didn't have to go round muttering platitudes," thought Neil as he closed down his station and followed Geoffrey back to his office.

* * *

"I still have lots of friends and associates from my past career days," explained Geoffrey, "I rarely call in any favours but, now and again, they have their uses. So I had a bit of a chat with an old chum who works for the other Office."

Neil nodded. He could have guessed that '6' were involved in some way.

"You're absolutely right to be sensitive to their feelings. Twitchy lot, they are. They seem to think the world is their oyster and look on us as a batch of amateurs. They weren't at all amused when they heard that we have been trampling on their patch. Quite cross, in fact. Never mind, they'll get over it."

"Tricky," Neil sympathised, "That's mainly why I came to see you. How did you manage to smooth their crumpled feathers?"

"Simple really, Explained that my work load was horrific and I had to pass the job to one of my subordinates who was less experienced."

"Thanks a bunch, Geoffrey. I really needed that!"

"We all have to make sacrifices for the job, Neil. Anyway, I digress. My chum apparently has a cosy relationship with the local chief of police in Nice."

"Not sure that's going to help us," said Neil, a touch too aggressively. "The local gendarmerie put their number twelves all over the night club. Just so they can get to talk to the manager. Hardly subtle, is it?"

Geoffrey sighed.

"I do wish, Neil, that you would occasionally think before you jump to conclusions. Now, do you want me to go on or not?"

"Sorry, Geoffrey, for some odd reason this case, trifling though it is, is getting to me. Somewhere, someone out there knows who shot our agent and why. I can't believe we should give up at this stage."

"Nor can I, Neil, nor can I. But I do think that our link with '6' and their link to the local police is the way forward. Do we know exactly when the meeting between Vince and Ryan took place?"

"We know roughly when Merrington had his talk with François. François, if I remember this correctly, hadn't seen Vince for some time but, whenever he did it must have been only a day or so after that meeting took place. Merrington told me that Vince was still seething about "bloody Americans" the last time he met François."

"Right," agreed Geoffrey, "but we must be more precise than that. We can't ask the French to find a needle in a haystack; I don't have that much trust in them! Maybe a needle in a shed load of hay, though. Someone needs to talk again to this Frenchman. What was his name again?"

"François," said Neil patiently. "Sounds as though we need Merrington again."

CHAPTER FIFTEEN

By mutual consent they agreed that the pub was not the best place to continue discussions, particularly as Tom had the night off from serving behind the bar. So they repaired to Richard's cottage where Buster gave them all an enthusiastic welcome.

"I think we are all agreed that Oliver Brady is the only person who can fill in the gaps." said Richard. "Personally I am against Sian questioning Helen du Plessis again. She is probably regretting saying as much as she did anyway and I cannot see how we can push her any further without becoming downright intrusive, and that's not what we are about. No offence, Sian, as I am sure you were totally discreet."

"Oh, I quite agree with you, but I get the impression from what both she and Dad said that Brady is beyond the stage of having a meaningful conversation with anyone."

Tom had been listening in silence, until now basking in the rays of a late afternoon sun as it streamed across Richard's living room.

"I am not so sure," he said, "I do agree with you both that the answers lie with Brady and not with Mrs. du Plessis. But look at it this way; even if Brady was able to have a meaningful conversation with one of us, which apparently he is not, how do we get to meet him? None of us know him. I have probably been here the longest of all but until Sian's father mentioned his name I had no idea he existed. We can't just 'phone him up to have a chat, completely out of the blue. He doesn't know us and we don't know him."

"And your point is?" queried Richard.

"My point is that there is only one person who can easily get to see Brady and that is your Dad, Sian. Peter regularly sees him on his rounds, he said so himself."

During the silence that followed Buster impatiently muzzled his master's hand and wagged his tail reminding Richard he had yet to have his evening walk.

"I think I agree with you Tom," said Richard, "but can we really bring Peter into this? Hasn't he got enough on his plate?"

"Oh, come on Richard; he is not that busy and I bet he'd love to be involved," said Sian, "as long as it does not cross any ethical boundaries, that is."

"Well, I suggest that is for him to decide." Tom concluded, "I think you should talk to him straightaway, Richard."

"Oh, do you, young man? Perhaps I will at that!"

*   *   *

Peter readily accepted Richard's invitation for an evening dog walk.

"I am forever telling my patients to take more exercise while I convince myself that walking to and from the surgery every day is good enough and allows me a large gin and tonic while watching television." he said, "As if!"

They walked through the village with Buster straining at the leash, anxious to be free to run, sniff and roll. They turned down an overgrown footpath and came out to a vista of fields; some with heads of corn already ripening; others lying fallow as part of the crop rotation and others a mass of yellow rape.

"I wonder if leaving the EU will mean we can get rid of this damned rape," exclaimed Peter, "I admit to not being a farmer, or one particularly interested in things agricultural, but I do question whether the powers that be realize the misery rape causes in mid-summer to hay-fever sufferers and those with asthmatic problems. Get rid of it I say and free up my waiting room!"

Richard smiled at the doctor. "I am sure a number of farmers would disagree with you, Peter, but I have to say I don't particularly like the mass of intense yellow. It is in your face, somehow, and a country mile away from the picture of Wordsworth's daffodils."

As they spoke Buster gave a yelp and took off in pursuit of a hare which had momentarily stopped for a face wash. The two men idly watched, as they knew Buster had no chance whatsoever of catching the hare.

"May I ask you a favour Peter?" Richard was uncertain how to approach the subject but decided not to prevaricate. "I know you mentioned to Tom and Sian that Oliver Brady is one of your patients and he is not terribly well at the moment."

Peter stopped abruptly and turned to the other man.

"I am not sure what this favour is Richard, but I hope you realise that I will in no way discuss anything to do with my patients in general or Oliver Brady in particular. I was enjoying this walk Richard; don't spoil it!"

"I know Peter. I know and the last thing I would want is to intrude in that way; but at least let me explain our predic-ament and how you may be able to help."

So he explained in detail where their search had led them so far; what Sian had been told by Helen du Plessis and how they sought to find out more without causing hurt or upset to anyone.

"It seems to us," he said, "that the only person who could help us to the next stage is Oliver Brady. But it would be wrong for one of use to attempt to talk to him. You, on the other hand, see him regularly."

They resumed walking, Peter in deep thought, Richard quietly along-side hoping against hope that he had not cause offence and Buster realizing it was near his meal-time and that it was politic to stay close to his master.

"I have listened very carefully to everything you have told me," Peter broke the silence that had become slightly un-comfortable between them. "You have realised that I cannot and will not breach any con-fidences between doctor and patient. That said it is safe to make some generalised comments about dementia.

"The condition is at present irreversible and early symptoms are loss of memory and difficulty in constructing sentences. As time goes by these problems worsen and other effects develop including immobility and general ill-health. It is distressing to witness and impossible to treat, other than by palliatives.

"Interestingly though, the memory loss in the earlier stages seem to relate to the immediate past. A patient may not remember what he had for breakfast but can remember details which took place months or years ago. We have yet to understand the cause for this although it seems likely that memories are stored in the brain in different compartments and that the memory loss reflects the progression of the disease. The memory will worsen in time, of course but trials have shown that certain events are retained in startling clarity by some patients even when the dementia has taken hold. On balance and for obvious reasons the mind tends to reject unpleasant events but retains happier moments."

He paused and Richard said, "Thank you for that Peter" and Peter smiled at his friend, all anger now dispersed.

"As to Mr. Brady," the doctor continued, "it is true that I do visit him at least once a week and that breaks no confidences. There is not a lot I can do for him at the moment and I am glad that Mrs du Plessis will remain with him until her services are no longer required. I hope that I can be of some comfort to him and we chat about all sorts of things, or rather I chat and he listens. But occasionally something I say will create a spark and he will talk about his past life not necessarily coherently but often with animation. I must admit I don't always pay the closest attention as I am just content to see his face light up as it comes back to him.

"And that is all I am prepared to say about Oliver Brady, Richard, but now you have told me your side of this intriguing story I will do this for you. I will listen closely if and when he has lucid moments and now I have had your input I will listen for any clues about his life when he was at XL. Whether I relay that information to you is a matter for me and me alone. I repeat Richard I will not break patient confidentiality and you must never ask me to do so."

"Of course not Peter, and thank you."

*   *   *

Richard had resigned himself to not hearing from the doctor for at least another two weeks, and he agreed with Tom and Sian that there was nothing more they could do in the meantime. Indeed they shared the view that if Peter was unable, or perhaps unwilling, to disclose anything of interest out of his meetings with Brady then possibly the mystery would never be solved.

Peter's 'phone call a few days later therefore came as a complete surprise. Richard listened carefully to every-thing Peter said and decided, in all fairness, that he should bring the other two into the picture.

The three of them met at Richard's cottage in time for a welcome morning coffee. The sky was leaden and the temperature had dropped and irregular showers dis-couraged any thoughts of country walks.

"In April I remember thinking it was more like mid-winter and now in June it seems like April! Why do we live in this dreadful climate?" questioned Sian as she shook her umbrella dry at the front door.

"Because tomorrow the sun will probably shine, the countryside will come alive and you will be glad you don't live anywhere else." said Richard in a buoyant mood.

They gathered in the sitting room with the glow of table lamps lifting the gloom caused by the overcast skies and the overhanging thatch.

"We may have something to work on following your Dad's involvement, Sian. It could be something or it could be nothing but I think there is a glimmer of hope. Peter cannot make it today but is happy for me to have this meeting."

Peter had, it seemed, thought more deeply about his past meetings with Brady. He was disinclined, he had said in his slightly pompous way, to lead his patient by any form of questioning, but he had realised that to wait for Brady to say something meaningful was like waiting for a No 99 bus to arrive. So he dug back in his memory when Brady had talked both rationally and sensibly. Nothing came to him at first but then suddenly, as he was dead-heading roses in his garden, he remembered Brady telling him with great humour about a firm's cocktail party which became a complete shambles when two important guests fell out in a spectacular way with one throwing the contents of his glass over the shirt front of the other with the compliment duly returned and all hell breaking loose. Brady thought it immensely funny explaining that rescue came in the form of a diminutive pretty young woman who scolded both of them to the extent that the contestants were totally shamefaced into apologising to all and sundry. Apparently Brady and the woman became friends after that, saying to the doctor: "By God, she was pretty, even I could see that! Amy Johnson was her name; she ran the Nightshelter in Winchester, by God she was pretty!" Brady had reflected but moved on to some totally unrelated incident and then lapsed into silence. As far as Peter could recall he had not mentioned the woman again.

Peter could see no harm in relaying all this to Richard, which Richard now relayed to Tom and Sian.

"Well," said Tom, "where is this leading us?"

"Goodness knows," replied Sian, "but at least we have someone who knew Oliver Brady when he was running XL Solutions. If she is still alive!" she added as an afterthought.

"We should be able to find that out easily enough, but why does that name Amy Johnson ring a bell?" questioned Tom.

"Well before your time, both of you," Richard answered, "Amy Johnson was a famous woman aviator before the last war. She died in the 1940s in a mysterious flying accident but she was very well known to her generation. I think she was the first woman to fly solo from England to Australia but anyway she is certainly not the woman at the party, though it could be why Brady remembered the name and equally why Peter recalled Brady talking about her."

"Surely it is worth checking with the Nightshelter?"

"There may be a slight problem there," cautioned Richard, "your father thinks he should be the one that follows it up."

"Does he now?" said Tom angrily, "we take him into our confidence and now he wants to run the show! I think not!"

Sian coloured with embarrassment; It was her father he was criticising.

"Hold on, young man!" Richard could see Sian's reaction, "I should remind you that I instigated this whole thing. I did not have to include anyone else but I did and so far I am pleased that I did. Don't make me change my mind!"

"Anyway," Sian was anxious to cool tempers, "I think Dad has a point."

"So do I, "Richard agreed. "he said that as Brady's GP he has the right to investigate things on his patient's behalf, whereas we have not. If he is happy to do so then I think we should be grateful to him for volun-teering."

"Yes," mumbled Tom sheepishly, "sorry about what I said."

"Don't worry about it, Tom, I was your age once."

CHAPTER SIXTEEN

Smithson had been instructed by Neil to maintain contact with Merrington and this instruction had been issued when the Office first used Merrington as an occasional agent on the Mougins affair.

Smithson was a well trained, meticulous operative who understood his own limitations and was content with his job, recognising that future promotion was extremely unlikely. He had met Merrington at irregular intervals either by the occasional telephone call or in a variety of non-descript cafés or bars dotted around the Winchester area.

His latest meeting had been at Neil's request, as a prelude to asking Merrington to revisit the south of France to make contact with François.

"To my surprise Merrington insisted that it was probably unnecessary to visit Biot again, as he had François' mobile number," he explained to Neil. "He was even able to produce the card given to him by François. I tried to talk him out of it but he insisted he was fully aware of the dangers of an unscrambled phone call and, to be honest, I am more than happy that he knew what was at stake here."

Neil sucked his teeth.

"Let's hope you are right then," he said, "as long as he avoids mentioning places or identifying people."

"I didn't have to tell him," Smithson said, "he told me! He is intelligent enough. I like him and he is no novice in this game."

"I agree. Anyway you have the authority to make that decision. Let's keep everything crossed and wait to hear how he gets on."

"Now that will require a meeting" said Smithson.

*   *   *

"François, c'est Richard., ça va. Can we speak in English?"

"But of course. Have you any news for me?"

"Possibly. I only need one thing from you at this moment though. Will you help?"

"Maybe, maybe not. You will remember, however, that everything

90

has a price?"

"Yes, I know, but all I need is for you to confirm the exact date of the meeting we talked about. The meeting between my friend and the American. You know the one I mean?"

"Bien sûr mon ami. Before I answer that the price is that you tell me about your friend; am I likely to see him again?"

"No, François, you are not. I am sorry."

"I think I understand. That is bad news for me."

"Of course."

"I will tell you the date. It was the 23rd February this year. Exactement"

"Are you sure about that?"

"Certainment. It was my birthday, I always remember my birthday! Let me say this Richard. I understand that you cannot tell me anything more and I think I know why. But although we come from different worlds, you and I, we have certain values that we both hold. In these circumstances I will tell you that if I can help in any way I will and without any need for you to pay!"

"That is extremely gracious François and very humbling, Thank you so much."

"Ce n'est rien. Just let me know."

"Of course. Just one more thing, François."

"Oui?"

"Joyeux Anniversaire."

*   *   *

Smithson said to Merrington.

"I've got some news for you, following your chat with François."

"I was wondering what was happening; It's been over a week now!"

"Mmm. I can assure you that a lot has happened in that week. The main thing you should know is that the American Ryan does not exist."

"What?" Richard exploded, "Of course, he exists. There is no way François would have made it up!"

"No, I don't think he did. Not in the way you mean it. But that was not his name and he was not American."

Richard shook his head.

"I know you people work in mysterious ways but this is bordering on the ridiculous!"

"Hear me out!" said Smithson, "I will tell you all about it as I suppose, in a way, you are one of us now!"

"How kind," Richard could not keep the sarcasm from his voice. "I must admit I have not actually rolled up my right trouser leg yet but I have run my share of dirty deliveries!"

"We are not the bloody Masons," Smithson rejoined. "You know full well how much I can and can't tell you. Now, do you want me to go on or not?"

Richard nodded, not embarrassed in the slightest.

"We were able to get the French police to help us," Smithson went on, ignoring Merrington's raised eye-brows. "They were able to persuade the owner of Pub Bliss to release his videotape of the evening of 23rd February and for two days either side, just in case Francois did not know his own birthday."

Smithson smiled at his own joke.

"I suppose we can guess in what way he was persuaded," suggested Richard.

"I would not know," said Smithson, "but threatening to close the Pub if he did not comply might be one option! Anyway the tape has been couriered to us and is being actively worked on as I speak."

"You mean they were able to tape both Vince and Ryan, or whatever his name is?"

"Better than that. The tape also picked up what they said to each other. Just in the background, you know, but our lads are wizards on stuff like this. Practically every single bloody word!" he said triumphantly.

"Good God!" Richard could not conceal his excitement, "and what exactly did they say?"

"Not now Richard. In any case the lab boys have not quite finished their work yet."

Richard could scarcely contain himself, and then, "Hold on a minute," he said cautiously, "does this make sense? Vince was a trained operative and could have guessed a conversation late at night in a

92

public bar might be taped."

"Oh, Vince was a true professional," said Smithson, "he said nothing of any consequence and tried to stop the other man from talking, but unlike Vince he was definitely the worse for drink and clearly didn't give a damn who heard him!"

"Well I'll be damned," said Richard, "but what's all this about Ryan not being Ryan?"

"You'll have to hear the tape for yourself, Richard. Not here of course; I am afraid another trip to the Office. Shall we say in two days time?"

*   *   *

There were four of them in the small conference room. On the side table were coffee cups, drinking glasses, a tray of digestive biscuits and four definitely non-eco plastic bottles of water. Richard speculated that this had been the regulation quota for visitors from time immemorial and was not due to be changed in a hurry.

Neil said he thought it was appropriate that Richard should see and hear the tape so he could at least see the agent who had subsequently died.

"To start with we will run the video with no sound," said Smithson, and he signalled to the operator. The picture was grainy with the camera facing both men. One man was on a stool with a long drink in front of him.

"That's John Vince at the end of the bar in Pub Bliss and as you can see from the footage it is just before midnight, then you see the other man approaching him; that is the man you know as Ryan," he said addressing Merrington, "and yes it is 23rd February 2017 just as François told you."

"We have edited the film, which carries on for two hours, and highlighted the bits that matter; You can see that Vince is not keen to talk to Ryan; obviously he was enjoying a night-cap and had no wish for company."

At this point Smithson stopped the film. "The video is very long and, as you will hear, it is not that easy to pick up the conversation. We have therefore translated what we can into English which makes it easier for everyone."

"He means me," said Neil happily, "I do not speak a word of French, but I am quite fluent in Chinese," he added, mainly for his own benefit.

Smithson cast his boss a disparaging look and continued, mainly addressing Merrington.

"In front of you is an envelope with a copy of the English translation – please don't look at it yet as I would like you to hear part of the video first."

The film was run back to the beginning and restarted, this time with the sound added.

Although the sound had been amplified by the engineers the background noise was indistinct, indicating that the pub had few customers at that time of night.

It also seemed as though the bartender only returned spasmodically, mainly to check on the state of Vince's drink. When Ryan took his seat alongside Vince there was a brief exchange in French but too faint for the audience in the room to interpret.

"The engineers have done their best, and were able with the help of a lip reader to hear and interpret these early exchanges. It's all in the translation, but, in outline, Ryan is saying "Do you mind?" as he takes his stool alongside Vince and Vince, with extremely bad grace says, "If you have to!" or words to that effect. Vince then tries to ignore Ryan but Ryan, obviously already fairly drunk by then, shouts for the bartender and orders a Ricard for himself. When it arrives he gulps it down neat and promptly orders another. This continues for a while, with Ryan trying to engage Vince in conversation and Vince trying unsuccessfully to ignore him. Eventually Vince gives up and in desperation turns and asks the man his name. This is the bit I want you to hear Mr Merrington"

The tape is run through until Vince turns on his stool and angrily shouts at Ryan,

"Comment t'appelles-tu?"

"*What's your name*?" Smithson quickly translates at they proceed.

"Moi? Je ne suis personne. Je suis un inconnu! Je suis rien! Je n'ai pas de nom! Je suis rien – compris? Rien. Absolument rien!"

"Me, I am a nobody. I am an unknown! I am nothing! I do not have a name, I am nothing, understand? Nothing. Absolutely nothing!"

"Dans ce cas Je vais vous appeler Ryan. Compris?"

"In that case, I will call you Ryan. Understood?"

"So you see Richard, Ryan is a Frenchman after all. Ryan is no more than a pseudonym." Smithson smiled at Merrington, gloating just a little.

"So what was all this about Vince shouting 'Bloody Americans!'" Merrington responded. "Don't tell me he did not say that either!"

"No, of course we're not," Neil intervened. "You will find it all in the translation which I read in advance of this meeting. If you don't mind we will leave the translation for you to read and, as they used to say in school, 'inwardly digest'. There is a lot to take in, I have to say, so tell our friend when you are finished. You will understand that you cannot make any notes nor have a copy. The translation in your envelope is to be handed back and it will then be destroyed. Sorry to be so James Bond-ish about it all but I am sure you understand."

"Well, if you can't be James Bond-ish, then I don't know who can!" said Richard with a smile, "But before you go, did you find out Ryan's actual name?"

"Yes," said Neil, "the French police have told us he is Marcel Autriche, aged thirty-nine. Once employed by their equivalent of MI5 but when they re-organised in 2014 he was made redundant. Apparently drifted around as low life on the fringes of the underworld getting in and out of trouble as a petty criminal. The DGSI tried to keep tabs on him but he didn't really come up on their radar and to a large extent he was left alone."

"So can the French Security not do us a favour and pick him up?" Richard queried.

Smithson gave a short laugh.

"Not really. On the 10th March he was found very dead in a ditch in the Nice outskirts. His throat had been cut and his fingernails had been removed, probably one by one, while he was still alive. There have been no arrests and none expected."

Merrington had an hour's train journey before he arrived at Winchester, long enough to mull over the almost unbelievable account of the meeting between Vince and Ryan. He could understand why both the tape and the translation were considered so sensitive and, in an odd way, he felt privileged to have been taken into 5's confidence. While he would have liked to have seen the whole video, the translation was itself breath-taking. He, like many others, had found the American elections to be incredible enough, but this! The world had gone mad. In Richard's view Vince could well have shouted "Bloody Americans; they reckon they know it all," as, faced in the same situation, he would have similarly re-acted. The problem was that the genie had been well and truly let out of the bottle and it was difficult to see what to do next.

Merrington turned it round and round in his mind and invariably came to the same conclusion. There was no obvious way forward. John Vince and Ryan had been killed at about the same time. Ryan's exact time of death was uncertain, but his body had been found within a day or so of Vince being shot on Wednesday 9th March. Obviously both deaths were connected and from what Ryan had told Vince, he, Ryan, knew far more than was good for him about an explosive political international plot. So presumably someone decided to shut Ryan up for good and it was known he had said far too much while in Vince's company so, he also, had to be killed. In any case with both of them dead there was no one left to ask, or so it seemed.

Richard sighed, he appreciated that what had been unearthed so far would cause at least three intelligence agencies to move the problem higher up the chains of command on a 'need to know' basis. "Best of luck with that one," he thought. Until he heard from them he could do no more.

He would have to return to his pathetic little problem in the village.

CHAPTER SEVENTEEN

"Sian, would you do me a favour?"

"I might. I only came up here for a cup of tea you know, Dad!"

"I know, I know, but the price of a cup of tea in this house is agreeing to do me a favour!"

"Even though I get it myself?"

"Even though."

Sian gave a theatrical sigh.

"Oh very well then. So what do you want me to do?"

"Become my secretary for the day and make a few 'phone calls."

"Depends on the salary!"

"I'll give you a smack on your legs if you refuse, just like I did when you were a youngster!"

"O.K. Only a pleasure when you put it that way."

"Good, now here is what I want you to do."

*   *   *

"I spoke to a charming lady who is currently the manager at the Nightshelter," said Sian. "Apparently they only moved to their current premises in 1988, so they would have some difficulty in checking their records before then."

"Fair enough, after all we are looking as far back as nearly 45 years ago! Didn't she question why we wanted to find Amy Johnson and on what authority?"

"Dad," said Sian patiently, "this is precisely why you employed me on such attractive terms, because you would have blundered in and put her back up straight away. Whereas I, one time failed journalist, was able to sweet talk her to the extent that she even sympathised with me for having you as a boss! Only joking, Dad! The fact that you are Oliver Brady's G.P. helped, although she did say she would need some kind of documentary proof before she could officially release information on past residents or staff."

"Understandable in this day and age," said Peter, "so where do we go from here?"

"She will check back in the records and 'phone me. If she finds anything that might help I am fairly sure that she will contact me again, but I think that's the time when you take over and meet her. Her name is Wendy Forester, by the way. Nice lady."

"Well done, secretary mine. Let's hope she does not leave it too long."

*   *   *

"Yes, she was a lovely lady!" said Peter, "No problems there, I am pleased to say."

"Who are we talking about now?" said Sian, "I get very confused about all the lovely ladies in your life."

"Very funny," said her father, "Mrs Wendy Forester, man-ager of the Nightshelter. I've been to see her and satisfied her about my provenance. Amy Johnson was the manager at the Nightshelter when they moved premises in 1988 and had been for at least twenty years before that. So, apparently, she is the one Oliver Brady lusted over!"

"Dad, really! I take it she is alive, then?"

"Very much so, according to Mrs Forester. Apparently Miss Johnson retired in 1995, when she was sixty-five, so she would now be eighty-eight and has been resident in a Winchester care home for the last ten years or so."

"Well I am fairly certain that at eighty-eight years of age either she would not remember a thing about Mr Brady or she won't be up to being grilled by you!"

"Wrong on both counts, so I have been told. Apparently Miss Johnson is as sharp as a tack and wears down all the other residents with her chatter and even finishes the Telegraph crossword each Saturday, before the other residents even get a look in!"

"Good luck then Dad, sounds as if you might need it!"

It turned out the care home was not in Winchester at all. Peter eventually tracked it down to a lovely old house in beautifully manicured grounds in a village some seven miles north-east of Winchester. The house had been owned by the same family for over two hundred years, he discovered, when he chatted to a friendly Pakistan man, who had bought the village shop when the previous owners had decided it was too much like hard work to make a living. Evidently the new owner was neither averse to hard work or long hours for a reasonable profit. The shop was clean, well stocked and well patronised.

As his wife was also available to serve, Javed, as he introduced himself, was happy to chat to Peter.

"I am told that the lady who owns the house has no children or close relatives to take over the care home when she dies, which is very sad. In truth though, I think that the business is not good. I have heard that each year that goes by she has to put more money into it to keep it going and I gather it is only half full these days. Very sad."

"Indeed," said Peter, "I believe it has a good reputation though. I do need to see someone there if I can."

"Then you should go now," insisted Javed. "It is nearly time for their afternoon tea. Quite a ritual with the English upper-class I believe!"

Peter laughed.

"Theoretically there is no such thing as the English upper-class any-more. We are all equal these days, or so I am told!"

"So I hear; if that is the case than that is also very sad. For the English gentry had a style which I admire. Good manners, a gracious way of living and respect for society's rules. Are these things now of the past?"

"I think you and I should have lived two hundred years ago Javed."

"Then we would never have met," Javed pointed out as Peter bade his farewell.

*   *   *

It could have come from a film set at Downton Abbey. Peter was thankful he had dressed in a jacket and tie, despite being a warm day in early June; so convinced was he that anything less formal would not be met with the same courtesy from Miss Olivia Hartingdon; lady of the house.

It was indeed tea time at the Manor, as evidenced by the number of elderly residents gathered in the lounge area with cake tiers on the tables in front of them together with porcelain cups and saucers and, of course, linen napkins.

"I will ask if Amy is available to see you," said Miss Hartingdon, having examined his visiting card with considerable care.

"She does not know me, nor I her," Peter explained, "one of my patients knew her many years ago and he thought he had lost touch. His state of health is such that he cannot unfortunately travel and indeed his memory is not what it used to be, but it would bring him great joy to learn of her continued existence."

It must be the place, thought Peter to himself. Five minutes in these surroundings and I find myself talking as if it was the turn of the century!

"I quite understand," said Miss Hartingdon, patting him reassuringly on the hand.

"Leave it with me, I will see what I can do."

Ten minutes later, when Peter had begun to think he was on a fool's errand, she returned.

"Amy will see you now," she said, "I am sorry I have been a little while but Amy does chatter on, I must say. She is having tea in the conservatory today. I can take you there, if you like."

"Please don't bother, you have done enough already. I can see the conservatory from here and I will find my own way."

"You can't miss her," said Miss Hartington, MBE.

*   *   *

He decided that she did not look like Amy Johnson. Not because he had any idea what she should look like but to his mind the sprightly, frail white haired lady looked for all the world to him like she should have been called Winifred Bird. It just suited her, he thought. She insisted immediately on seeing him that he should call her "Amy" however, so that dispelled that irrational thought.

As he had been warned, Amy Johnson could chatter. Interminably. For once she had a captive audience; someone who had not heard her life story before and she made the most of it.

Peter found it all very interesting but totally irrelevant to the real reason of his visit; when Amy's life story started to centre on things medical and she said "but of course you are a doctor, aren't you? Now what would you have diagnosed from my symptoms?" that he interrupted her mid-flow.

"Can you remember back to 1974 Amy? That is when you first met Oliver at his office cocktail party?"

"Oliver? Oliver who? Oh yes you said, Oliver Brady. I remember now. What do you mean do I remember 1974? Of course I do! I remember everything. Now who was that Oliver chap again?"

"You met him at a cocktail party when he was running a firm called XL Solutions. You were running the Nightshelter at the time and you were looking for a home for a refugee."

Amy's response was immediate and accusatory.

"What would you know about that?" she demanded.

Peter flustered, struggled for something to say, faced with a question which demanded an answer, and could only manage,

"How do you mean Amy? I only know what Oliver told me."

He realised that even that was untrue, Brady had certainly mentioned Amy but the suggestion she was involved with a refugee was sole conjecture on his part.

"What I do remember Amy, is that Oliver was smitten by you. I recall him saying, 'God she was so pretty,' not once, but at least twice."

"Really?" she said, visibly softening, "Well, perhaps I was, at that. In 1974, you say. Yes, I would have been in my mid forties, so though I say it myself, I was not short of admirers. I never married," she emphasised, "I had no need to and it seemed such a waste of time. Still does!"

"I am quite sure you had plenty of admirers at the time," Peter felt he had almost saved the day, " Indeed, I am sure you still do!"

He could not avoid her piercing look which unsettled him with its intensity.

"Come, come Doctor Jordan. Don't overplay your hand!"

He realised he had been caught out and he burst out laughing and Amy joined in with a girlish laughter which belied her eighty eight years. They each wiped their eyes and the surrounding residents, startled by the sudden mirth, settled back to their normal routine with no more unseemly interruptions.

"Now then, young man. Let's get back to business! I do remember that cocktail party and vaguely I recall Oliver. Nice man, a bit full of himself but then most men are, aren't they doctor?"

"I got the impression that you and he met quite a few times rather than just the once," ventured Peter, "he was certainly full of your praises!"

"There you go again. Either he or you are imagining things that just did not happen. Don't forget I was single, not unattractive and had my pick of the men I wanted. Oliver was just one of those men, despite what he might have said. The reason I was interested in him was work opportunities for some of the unfortunates who sought sanctuary at the Nightshelter. He ran a large prosperous firm and he had expressed an interest in charitable work."

"And the refugee?" pressed the doctor.

"One day I shall be interested to discover where you found out about the refugee. I rather doubt it was from Oliver himself," she said reflectively. "It has always been our secret. It had to be, as we were both guilty of breaking the law, but that was then, some forty years ago. I am sure it has all changed now."

"Why were you breaking the law?" Peter quietly asked, not wanting to intrude into the private reverie that was the memory of a remarkable lady in the twilight of her life.

He sat and listened as the years were rolled back so many decades as Amy recalled with remarkable clarity those events of the past.

It had been a particularly busy evening at the Nightshelter in the June of 1974. As always there was a desperate shortage of beds and it always upset her to turn away so many of the world's outcasts to fend for themselves as best as they were able. Although she sought to maintain complete impartiality in her dealings with the hopefuls who crowded the hostel, she had less sympathy for those who had succumbed too readily to drink and drugs and were abusive to her staff in their efforts to provide help and sustenance.

She therefore had little left in her well of human kindness when the policeman had pleaded with her to look after the dirty, hungry young man he had found wandering, lost and homeless, on the streets of affluent Winchester. Nonetheless she sat the stranger down in the corner of reception area, gave him a mug of tea and thanked the policeman. He told her he was Polish and although his broken English was not always easy to understand she became fascinated by the sad little story he had to tell.

She had managed to find him a spare bed, one that was always kept for emergencies, but although the office was now closed she decided to stay on, encouraging the man to complete the tale of his experiences.

She admitted to Peter she was attracted to the man despite his rough exterior.

"I could see he was not attracted to me," she told Peter, with a twinkle in her eye, "he had that slightly effeminate look about him which makes women want to look after him, if you know what I mean?"

"What was his name, Amy?"

"Something quite unpronounceable in Polish, but it sounded a bit like Frederick, I think. Anyway I called him Freddy. He can only have been in his twenties, if that. I think he had trained to be a chef, although I am not sure I always understood what he was saying," she laughed, "but I could understand enough to know that he had had a very hard life at such a young age."

She re-told how he had paid money he could ill-afford to be smuggled to Calais, and eventually hid un-noticed on a container lorry that found its way to Twyford; a village on the edge of Winchester. By this stage he was cold, hungry and in desperate need of a toilet. The lorry had stopped with the driver having been wrongly directed.

"He could hear a lot of shouting between the driver and a policeman," Amy explained, "If I understood Fred correctly the lorry should have been sent to Berkshire and not Hampshire. Did you know there is a Twyford in Berkshire as well as one in Hampshire? I certainly didn't and nor did the lorry driver, apparently. Anyway, with all the shouting and the presence of the police, Freddy took fright and managed to escape without being seen. He had been wandering the streets of Winchester for three nights before the policeman found him. "Three cold and wet nights I seem to remember."

"You talked about you and Oliver breaking the law, Amy. In what way?"

"Well obviously he was an illegal immigrant. The policeman who found him said as much and when I agreed to take him in he made it abundantly clear that the first thing I should do was to take him to a Police Station or at least report it. Well I was never going to do that!"

"Why ever not?"

"This poor lad was virtually in tears as he told me his story. He was terrified of the police; he had obviously had some bad experiences crossing Europe and he implored me not to report him.

"Anyway I did not agree with the law. Why should a poor frightened lad like this be put through yet another traumatic experience? What would have happened to him? Made to apply to stay in this country; knowing full well his chances of being accepted were virtually nil. He was young for his years and scared witless by a country he did not understand other than the fact that it had to be better than the one he had left."

Peter was beginning to understand the inner strength of this remarkable old lady.

"So you were prepared to stand up and fight the establishment for the sake of this young lad?"

"Don't build me up to someone I definitely was not," said Amy. "I was no Joan of Arc, nor even an Emmeline Pankhurst. There are times when you have to fight for what you believe in but this was no big deal. All I did was to persuade a wealthy businessman, who seemed to fancy me, into giving young Fred some sort of job, recognising of course that he was an illegal immigrant."

"So, Oliver knew he was breaking the law?"

"Of course he did. What started out with me fluttering his eyelashes at him and occasionally giving him a glance of my cleavage ended up with Oliver and Freddy falling for each other and making my presence totally irrelevant! This business about men being gay is something I have never understood, but it obviously suited them so who was I to care?"

"So, did you stay in touch with them after that?"

"No, not really. To be honest they only had eyes for each other. I remember Oliver telling me it was not appropriate to employ him in the firm but he was taking him in as a live-in companion. In fact this made a great deal of sense as apparently Freddy was a very competent chef! Oliver did ask me not to mention it, which suited me. I think he tried to avoid people knowing about it altogether but you have as much chance keeping a secret in a village like that as I have of seducing a man at my age!"

"Oh, I don't know Amy; You have me totally entranced!"

Which made them both erupt in laughter once again and they did not really care if it upset the other residents.

CHAPTER EIGHTEEN

"I was wondering if I should get a season ticket to here from Winchester," Richard said. "Alternatively, perhaps I could stay in your penthouse flat for a while?"

"Not very funny!" rebuked Smithson, "you want to thank your lucky stars you don't work here all the time. I am beginning to wonder if my wife even recognises me."

"Could we start the meeting?" Neil was not in the mood for flippant pleasantries at this time of the morning, or indeed at any time.

"Thank you for coming Richard. As you will have realised the Mougins affair has stopped being a minor irritation and has reached new levels. We now need to look on you more as permanent staff rather than a casual agent. Otherwise we will have to preclude you from some, if not all of our meetings and that in the circumstances would be inconvenient."

Smithson laughed, inappropriately.

"That means you can come to the Christmas party, Richard! Wow!"

Neil sighed

"If we can just be serious for a moment, As I am sure you have realised, that video showing the meeting between Vince and Ryan has opened a can of worms. The suggestion that behind it all may be a third party willing to hire guns for political ends is bad enough. Far worse is the implication that all this took place without any of our agents picking up any vibes whatsoever; which mean that we could have been faced with an international incident with, to put it mildly, world wide ramifications."

Smithson interrupted. "I think we all realise the seriousness of the issue, but the assumption is that these wild allegations are valid, or at least contain more than a germ of truth and we don't know that. Least not as far as I know. Or are you going to tell me something different?"

"No," admitted Neil, "I am not. What I can tell you is that the issue will have to be discussed at the highest levels, by which I mean our own DG and the Head of '6'."

"I don't follow," said Merrington, "I can see why there should be concern and there should be questions asked about the failure of security organisations to pick up the scent before now. Nonetheless we are now on the case, so to speak, and it should be relatively easy for us to hunt it down and dispose of it quickly, efficiently and above all, locally."

"And surely the CIA and the French have to come into this, don't they?" Smithson queried.

"All valid questions gentlemen. Perhaps I have not spelt it out as well as I could. Let's summarize the facts shall we? If we take Ryan's outburst seriously, and it is a big 'if', then someone or somebody came to Nice representing a serious chunk of American cash, which for the moment we will guess was Democrat money, for the purpose of assassinating Donald Trump on his presidential visit to Paris on 14th July this year. It is now the 20th and it has not happened so we can assume that either they failed or decided not to go ahead."

"Can I stop you there, for a moment?" asked Richard. "If Ryan's drunken outburst can be taken at its face value, then Mr Big – in other words whoever represents the American money – seems to have made some sort of direct contact with Ryan. In that case, it seems to show at the best, naivety and, at the worst, total ineptitude. The man had been chucked out of DGSI and effectively become a petty criminal. Would you have touched him with a barge pole for what was a difficult, dangerous and delicate assignment like this? It does just not make any sense to me and I do not understand why Mr Big should be operational in Nice. The assassination, if there was to be one would have been in Paris, for God's sake, not on the Rivieria in the south of France!"

"I wouldn't like you to think we haven't already thought of that," Neil's put-down was gentle but a put-down nonetheless.

"The biggest problem in all of this is the fact that the two people who could have given us the answers are both dead. Of course what you say makes all the sense in the world but there are other factors to be considered.

Firstly it is not impossible that Ryan's name was leaked to Mr Big by an existing member of DGSI. At the time Ryan was effectively made redundant in 2014 he was recorded as a qualified marksman and was well liked by his colleagues. Possibly, and I must say possibly, someone might have thought he was doing Ryan a favour by suggesting him for the job. As you can imagine the French would be horrified at the suggestion but you can't take it off the table.

Secondly, for all we know the American element in all of this could have been extremely amateurish. It does not have the feel of something professional and competent and if that is the case it would have explained the approach to a totally unsuitable operative like Ryan.

Thirdly, the apparent advantage of Nice, rather than Paris, could be the fact that a disproportionate section of Algerian nationals live in the south of France with a worrying number of illegal immigrants prepared, no doubt, to consider hiring themselves and their armoury out to the highest bidder."

"Apparently it is American money that could be behind all this, so surely you should be talking to US security?" questioned Smithson, aggressively.

"I am not sure where this is all leading us," said Merrington, "where is the sensitivity in all of this?"

"Thank you Richard, sensitivity is the key to everyone's approach in this," said Neil, "Look at it this way. The proposed assassination did not take place. The two who were, by accident or design, in the know are both dead. So if the matter is considered closed no harm is done.

"On the other hand, what happens if we insist on pursuing this further? We would need to inform the CIA who no doubt would need to inform their Government; we would need, with the help of the French, to seek out all contacts of Vince and Ryan and, in short, all security would be totally blown. In no time at all the world's press would pick up the story and overnight headlines would be about the Democrats plan to kill the President on French soil. The President may not be killed by a bullet but the repercussions could be just as lethal."

Neil paused, waiting for a reaction from the two men.

"So is it the idea to do nothing, to hush it up and, in other words, not even to inform the French or the Americans?" asked Smithson, incredulously.

"It is one option." Neil picked his words carefully.

"And not even try to find the killer of one of our own agents?" spluttered Merrington.

"As I say, it is one option. In this business, Richard, one has to accept that there may be casualties of war. Vince may be one of those, I am afraid."

"It stinks." Richard was angry.

"I agree." said Smithson.

"Gentlemen, we will reconvene this afternoon at three o'clock. Discuss it between yourselves, if you wish, but obviously not anyone else. I make one further point. The final decision will be made at a higher level than mine. As we all realise, ours is a dirty business."

"But not necessarily an immoral one," said Richard.

*   *   *

Smithson fetched two cups of coffee from the machine and placed one in front of Merrington.

"Richard, circumstances seem to have thrown us together on this one. Time to be less formal, I suggest. My first name is William or, if you prefer, Bill."

"Not Willie then?" Richard asked impishly.

"No, I don't think so, do you? Anymore than I would call you Dick!"

They laughed together, at ease in each others company.

"I've always known you as Mr Smithson," Richard said, "If you remember that was how you first introduced yourself. So may I ask what is your actual name?"

"It is Smithson, believe it or not. At the time I couldn't think of anything else. One thing I learnt very quickly in this job – tell the truth whenever possible as you are less likely to be a tripped up at a later stage."

"I take it that neither of us are happy with the idea of letting sleeping dogs lie on this one, are we?"

"It's a load of bollocks isn't it? Neil bounced that idea at us just to get a reaction. Apart from anything else could we really leave both the French and Americans out of the loop? There would be hell to pay when it all came out, as it certainly would one day, be sure of that."

"Agreed," said Richard, "although I can see the superficial attraction of the idea. The problem surely is we don't know how much store to place on the ramblings of a drunken embittered man. If it is ninety per cent true it is frightening."

"Let's face it, if only ten per cent is true it is still scary enough," Bill pointed out.

"I can't believe that Ryan hadn't made his feelings known to other people, in other places before he met Vince. We need far more information before we can do anything, which, curiously, leads us back to Neil's crackpot idea of doing nothing – mainly because we could otherwise stir up a hornets' nest."

"That is the point isn't it?" countered Richard. "It would seem we are damned if we do and damned if we don't. In any case if it is agreed we must dig a little further then surely it will be out of our hands? After all this is really '6' territory and they, of all people, must have trained operatives in France who can ferret around with the least disturbance. With due respect Bill, if you were in charge would you really let either of us blunder in and ask questions in our dodgy French accents?"

"And there I was thinking my French accent was a product straight out of the Sorbonne," Bill complained light heartedly. "No, of course you are right, but I would warn you that there is no love lost between our side and the snotty nosed buggers who think that God is very lucky that they are on his side. I'll tell you now, Richard, that the Office will scrap like hell not to pass this onto '6', but you make a good point. The French won't be very happy either, if they are left on the side lines while we swan around their country. I think Neil might have something when he wondered whether Ryan could have been given the nod by an old pal who still works for the DGSI. That really would rattle their cage!"

"Hold on a moment," said Merrington, "I have just had an idea."

CHAPTER NINETEEN

"So we are gradually putting the jigsaw together," observed Tom. "We now know that Freddy was an illegal Polish homosexual immigrant employed as live-in lover–cum-housemaid by the then boss of XL Solutions."

"I can't believe you just said that!" exclaimed Sian. "That was a totally racist and homophobic comment, Tom. I am surprised at you and a bit shocked, to be honest."

"Well thank you, Sian," replied Tom with some force, "that is the trouble with this PC world of our's these days. Let's analyse what I just said, shall we? Firstly being here without a permit means Freddy was here illegally. Next we gather that he was born and lived in Poland, which in my book makes him Polish. Thirdly he was the boss's live in lover which by my book makes him homosexual, but maybe I have got that wrong! Fourthly he looked after the house and cooked meals for his master. In this gender specific age I am sure that he cannot be called a house-boy, or come to that, a house-anything. What he did makes him more of a house-maid to me, until someone can find a word that is acceptable to the digitally inspired politically correct community which apparently rules us these days, despite the fact that they still have to form a government."

Sian stood open-mouthed and shocked.

"I've just seen a side of you that I would never have guessed existed, and I do not like it, Tom."

"Well live with it. I was probably born in the wrong century any-way."

"Yes, I think you were Tom!"

The row ceased abruptly as her father came into the room.

"Now what am I interrupting? You can cut the atmosphere in here with a knife!"

"Don't worry about it Dad," Sian had quickly regained her com-posure and put on a bright smile, "I thought you were going to see Richard and bring him up to date?"

"No, I gather he is on his way back from London. He had a business meeting there."

"So, where do we go from here?" Tom made every effort to carry on as normal.

"I have told you both about my meeting with Amy," said Peter, "but we still haven't solved the problem of the headstone. We at least know when Freddy arrived and in what circumstances but not a great deal after that. Amy had vaguely heard that Freddy was no longer with Oliver Brady but she had virtually lost touch with them both by then. She did say though that she had heard Oliver has retired and was not in great health."

"It sounds as if the only person who can help us is Oliver Brady himself," said Tom.

"Maybe, Tom, but medically speaking it is not a good idea to raise such an emotionally charged subject with him. Having said that I am not really sure what we can do now. Did Freddy die in 1994 and if not, what did happen?"

"Hang on, Dad," interrupted Sian, "you have already established that 1974 was the date Freddy arrived here, and as Richard said some time ago, it doesn't follow that the other year on the headstone, 1994, was the year of his death any more than 1974 was the year of his birth."

"No, I know that," Peter was irritated, mostly with himself, "I am just so against talking with Brady even if that is the only way forward."

"So, don't," said Tom, "If it feels wrong to do it then it probably is wrong. There must be some other way. Let's look at this a bit more logically, If he did not die in 1994 when did he die? Does it necessarily follow there is a body in the grave where the headstone is? Even if there is a coffin, do we know what it contains?"

"Gruesome thought," said Peter.

"On the contrary, If there is no coffin or there is no body then the last thing it is, is gruesome!"

"No, I didn't mean it that way. It is a gruesome thought to open up graves whatever we may find. In any case none of that would be possible without police involvement, coroner's inquest, church authority's permission, etc., etc.!"

"Perhaps we have reached the point where we should be involving the police?" Sian suggested.

"And say what?" asked Tom, "that 'there is a headstone in the churchyard but we don't know if there is a body there, but if there is, it could be the body of an illegal immigrant who used to work years' ago for a man who is now suffering from terminal dementia?' Any bets on what sort of reaction we would get? 'Well yes sir, that sounds very important and precisely the sort of mystery the police are here for and we have plenty of time and would love to spend the taxpayers' money on this. We will get straight onto it, sir!'?"

"Don't be silly Tom; now you are just being absurd!" The embers from their previous row had, it seemed, yet to be extinguished.

"Why don't we see what Richard has to say?" Peter was determined to act as peacemaker, "he should be here by tomorrow"

*   *   *

"Sian! I guessed it was you!"

Sian had been lost in thought as she made her way home after the fruitless meeting at her father's house and she turned at the sound of the voice to see Helen du Plessis waving to her.

"Helen, how good to see you again! Sorry, I was somewhere else, if you know what I mean. Very discourteous of me, sorry!"

"Don't apologise Sian, I am just pleased you still recognised me. I kept meaning to give you a ring – but you know how it is – the older you get the more quickly time passes!"

Sian laughed.

"At this rate we'll end up apologising for apologising," she said, "To be honest I hesitated phoning you as I could never be certain you would be the one to answer, if you understand me?"

"I know exactly what you mean, Sian. Although I am not sure Oliver is even up to answering the 'phone these days."

"Things no better then?"

"'Fraid not, but then again I did not expect them to be. It is just a downward path from now on, you know. Still, it is good to see you. You must tell me what has been happening to you over the past few weeks?"

"Amongst other things, I am now a property owner," said Sian proudly. "I've flown the nest, so to speak. In fact I was on my way there now. Why don't you come and have a cup of tea and I will tell you all about it?"

Helen glanced at her watch.

"Why not? I am not expected back yet and anyway I left Oliver asleep. He always goes to bed in the afternoon and he won't be waking up for an hour or so. So, yes that would be nice."

They made their way to the small ground floor flat that was Sian's pride and joy and Helen made all the appropriate noises of appreciation.

They sat outside on this warm summer's day, shaded by a large parasol, and admired the immaculately cut lawns which spread out in front of them.

"Is this all yours?" Helen asked incredulously.

"No, of course not," Sian giggled, "all the flat owners can use the grounds as a condition of the lease. One of the flats is currently vacant and the other is occupied by an elderly couple who never apparently venture outside. So for the time being it is all mine. Well, not quite, but you know what I mean."

"And very pleasant it is too," said Helen, "and your father, the GP, how is he? We used to see him regularly but I think it is a few weeks now since he last called."

"Oh, he is fine, but the practice seems to have grown recently which takes up most of his time. That is probably why you have not seen him recently, but I will remind him to fit you in. So Mr. Brady is not doing too well then? I am particularly sorry for you, it must be very depressing."

"Well, yes and no. Physically he seems to be fine and is very good at taking his medication. I have no problem in getting the repeat prescriptions from the surgery so there is no point in bothering the doctor. It is the gradual collapse of his mind which is so distressing, although your father did say this would happen. It is all a question of time I suppose."

"Nonetheless it sounds as though a visit from my Dad is, if not overdue, at least due fairly soon. I will mention it to him very diplomatically, don't worry!"

"Thank you. I would like a chat with him if that is possible. I am getting worried about things Mr Brady has been saying."

"Oh dear," sympathised Sian, "can you tell me, or would you rather not?"

"I will speak to your father about it, if that is all right with you?" Helen said. "I am sure it is something or nothing and just part of his illness, but it does bother me when he talks about how he deliberately injured some-one. Anyway I have already said too much but I would appreciate it if the doctor would call."

"Of course," said Sian, "in the meantime I insist that you try my home made fairy cakes."

*   *   *

Peter and Richard decided they would meet without extending an invitation to either Sian or Tom. As Richard said, "You and I are old enough to exercise our right of seniority now and again and, in any event, Sian is not talking to Tom, and Tom has the night off anyway."

So they found two leather armchairs which had seen far better days but were comfortable enough, ordered two pints of bitter and sat in a quiet corner of the bar, awaiting delivery of their order. Tom's replacement turned out to be young, female and remarkably pretty, and after she had delivered the drinks and returned to the bar Richard commented that he did not really mind that Tom had the night off.

"I think both of us can claim to be of an age when we are no longer considered to be any danger to the fairer sex..." Richard opined.

"...and as a consequence can harbour the most erotic thoughts without giving any cause for concern!" Peter finished,. "Here's to us, anyway."

"Cheers," said Richard.

The first pint lasted them both long enough for Richard to be brought fully up to date on 'The Curious Case of the Headstone', as they had now decided to call it.

"And finally," said Peter, "the most intriguing development of all! Sian met Helen du Plessis, totally by accident. I know we agreed we would not approach her again but as luck would have it she hailed Sian in the street and they ended up having a cup of tea at Sian's flat."

"So," said Richard, "not earth shattering so far!"

"Do stop being so dismissive, Richard! You must relinquish your city upbringing and learn to live with us yokels! Seriously though; Helen du Plessis said that Oliver Brady, when his mind wanders, is berating himself for deliberately injuring someone in his past life. He can only mean Freddy, don't you see?"

"No," said Richard "not yet anyway. Did she specifically mention Freddy?"

"Not in so many words," Peter admitted, "apparently her exact words were that he had deliberately injured someone. That was when he was rambling about the past."

"So Sian and you have put two and two together and made five! You were the one who explained to me the devastating decline of someone with Alzheimer's and how it plays tricks with their memory. You even went so far as to say that things that tend to stick in the memory are happy events, not sad or bad ones. I would say that deliberately injuring someone falls into the last category wouldn't you?"

"Well yes," Peter admitted, "but Sian, Tom and I think that should it have been Freddy, and the injury did in fact result in death and that all happened in 1994 then we are closer to solving the puzzle, wouldn't you agree?"

"I think," said Richard ponderously, "that you, Peter, have been caught up in the excitement generated by the two youngsters and have lost your clinician's ability to diagnose. That is what I think! But having said all that it is an intriguing line of thought. I think we are some way off presenting a case to the jury though; there are far too many ifs and maybes!"

"It does seem a bit like Agatha Christie doesn't it?" said Peter, "Do we have a manslaughter, or indeed a murder on our hands? Listen to the next instalment, folks!"

"I am not sure there is a next instalment Peter. Coming down to earth have you thought about your next move? As a middle aged, down-to-earth, highly respected medical practitioner, I mean, not as a latter day 'snapper up of unconsidered trifles'."

"I'll tell you something Richard. Just now and again, just once, I would love to get away from the apparent superiority of my profession and our age and join the stupidity of youth. To prove that I am not getting any older, I suppose. Sad isn't it?"

"No, it is not, my friend. We all rage against the dying of the light in our own way. If I said, 'shall we have another pint?' what would you say?"

"I would say, no thanks. Two pints are enough for me!"

"There you are, then. You don't really want to relive your youth."

"No, I don't, but I don't really want to admit it."

"Me neither."

CHAPTER TWENTY

The silence in the room was palpable. They had not expected Neil to ask Geoffrey to be there and both Merrington and Smithson felt ill at ease and uncom-fortable in his presence.

Finally Neil shifted in his chair and looked directly at Smithson.

"I assume you have discussed this at some length? What is your opinion, Bill?"

"On balance, I think it is worth a go," said Smithson guardedly. "It's taking a risk, but then that's what we do, isn't it? As I see it, the skill is being able to see when it is all going pear-shaped and stopping it there and then."

"Pear shaped? Not sure I approve of your terminology, Smithson!" Geoffrey had not wanted to be at the meeting in the first place.

"He could have said 'tits up'," said Richard, who immediately wished he hadn't.

Neil intervened.

"Richard, the problem as I see it, is that whether it works or not it will be entirely up to your judgement. Forgive me for saying so, but you are not by any means our most experienced operator."

"I think Richard is a bit more than a rookie," Bill intervened. "More to the point, what he is proposing can only be carried out by him; there is no one else."

"I agree," Geoffrey's sudden endorsement was totally unexpected. "Neil, sort out the details; let me know how it develops. And Richard, try and make sure if does not go 'tits up', will you?"

*   *   *

"François! C'est moi, comme promis!"

"Richard, ça va? Are you now in Nice?"

"Yes, I would like us to meet as soon as possible. Where are you?"

"At Jules, but I can leave here at any time."

"Could we meet at my usual hotel in, say, thirty minutes time?"

"As long as you are paying!"

"Comme d'habitude , François, comme d'habitude."

*   *   *

The setting westerly sun still engendered sufficient heat to demand shade, and Richard chose an outside table in front of which was a large lemon tree, filtering the sun's rays to dapple the courtyard.

He saw François threading his way through the outside tables. Not for the first time he wondered how such a man could mingle so well with the disparate, unkempt and colourless crowd that frequented Jules place. He was of them, but not one of them, he decided.

As they were in Provence, they agreed on a bottle of vin rosé; once their glasses were charged and pleasantries exchanged Richard spoke.

"François, you have kept your word and helped me out when you could. To be frank, I never fully under-stood why you did, I know you were upset and angry at the death of your friend, but you took a risk for no reward!"

"You did not have to tell me that John was dead, Richard, I guessed it from your very manner. I also think that you are involved in some way with your Security Service, but I know others in your MI6 and our DGSI, and you are not like them. All the others I have met are hard, ruthless men who do not care who they hurt as long as they get what they want. You are not like them and if you are not careful you will be the one who gets hurt. That is why I helped you."

"Who are you François? I find it difficult to believe that you have much in common with some of the men I came across at Jules. I know you said you have respect for Jules, but he would seem to live, shall we say in the 'demi-monde'."

François laughed.

"Well perhaps, but in French 'demi-monde' means the fringes of society. Many of them are more 'la pegre', or 'le milieu'; a member of the underworld. Not all, but some. Not Jules and hopefully not me. Why are you so interested in who I am, Richard?"

"Because our work is unfinished. We still do not know who killed John, nor why. We have a number of leads but without going in to detail they are all politically very sensitive. Our more normal channels

119

of enquiry are not, in my view, open to us, but it angers me personally to think that we have to live with this uncertainty. I wondered whether we could find out more by using different channels."

"I see," François took another sip of wine and stared at Richard as if he was trying to explore his very soul.

"Richard, however odd it may all seem, everything depends on trust between us.

I, for my part, will tell you about myself and then you will have to make a judgement. Equally I need to know more about you before I am convinced that we can work together. If there is to be a deal, then it must be a two way deal. Do you agree?"

"Yes" said Richard without hesitation.

*   *   *

When François, in his own self deprecating way, started talking about his earlier days, the cadence of his cultured voice and what he had to say soon had Richard enthralled.

He could not have imagined a life so vividly in contrast with his own: François had been born in a small village outside St Etienne, to the south of Lyon, in what was an intensely Catholic community; François could only guess at the reaction when he was born as his mother was both alone and unmarried. He never knew his father.

"For all I know I could be Swiss – the border was not that far away! I was only five when my mother died so all I remember is being placed in a convent, to be looked after by the nuns. They tried their best, I know that, and I was treated no worse and no better than any other child."

The spell at the convent was not to last. His mother had been the beneficiary of a considerable sum of money, which François guessed to be from his unknown father, although this was never confirmed.

The local mayor then intervened, paid the convent a not inconsiderable sum of money and placed young François in expensive higher education establishments until he decided to walk out at fifteen.

"I was privileged, had a good education and with no-one to answer to decided to see the rest of the world. I explored the "demi-monde", as you put it, Richard, learnt how to paint in oils, lost my virginity in the most delightful way and became my own man; dependant on no-one and with a fortune in the bank!"

"But what makes you get up in the morning, François? What are your ambitions? You have so many years ahead of you. What are you going to do with them?"

"Before I answer that, tell me what you have done with your life, Richard. What has been making you get up in the morning all these years and when were you inspired by Sean Connery to try and save the British Empire?"

Richard laughed and shrugged his shoulders.

"What have I achieved in my fifty seven years on this planet? Not very much, if I am being honest. Sure, I have been materially successful in life and I don't think I have hurt too many people on the way up, but that's not how I would want to measure my life!"

"Why not? Many people would be proud to say that!"

"Maybe François, maybe. But away from my business life in insurance with all its highs and lows; the air-flights to all corners of the world, the hotels, the dramas and the disasters, I managed to screw up my private life, and that is where I hurt people and let myself down."

"And how come all this secret agent stuff? I don't want to know any detail or question you in any way, I am just interested in that side of your character."

Richard grinned.

"Don't worry François. I am not about to impart any state secrets! I somehow drifted into it, more by accident than design. I can't even remember how I was first approached; they are past masters at finding out more about you than you know yourself! Anyway enough of that. We were discussing your ambitions, remember?"

"Well you were, I am not so sure I was! In some ways I was hoping we could skip that part as I find it difficult to put into words and it is a little embarrassing!"

Haltingly and occasionally encouraged by Richard, François tried to set out his own philosophy of life. When he walked out of education at the age of fifteen it was with enough money to ensure that he would never have to work for his living. That made him uncomfortable and he was far too young to take it all on board. As luck would have it he stayed friends with his Housemaster who saw François as the child he never had and gradually the trust between them grew until François confided in him about his wealth.

"If ever I doubted my fellow beings; that man restored my belief with his kindness and total absolute honesty. He guided me along the way introducing me to financial advisors in whom I could trust implicitly because he could vouch for them and without taking even one sou of my money, even when pressed. He was not well off but I would offend him if I suggested I help in anyway. In the end, I gave up trying. He died when I was eighteen and I have never forgotten him. So, I did what every eighteen year old with money would do; travelled the world, tried cannabis and did not like it. Tried alcohol and decided I could take it or leave it and tried sex which I liked a lot."

"Of course you did," said Richard. "but did you do a job of work or just meander from one nightspot to another?"

"No, no," Francois protested, "that was all part of my growing up experience. I would never let it control my life. I was no idle playboy with too much money. I was learning about life, about people, both good and bad, about temptation, about joy, about sadness but above all how to recognise evil and good in people."

"Sounds a bit like Billy Graham to me. Do you get large crowds at your events?"

"I told you I would find it difficult to put into words, and now I have given you the impression that I am a 'petit saint' in some way!"

"A goody-two shoes?" laughed Richard, "No, of course I don't – far from it! But I still don't understand what you do with your life, unless you set up as a psychotherapist!"

"No, nothing like that," he said, "in some ways I have had the perfect life. I have thousands of friends all round the world. None of them know about my financial state; in fact you are almost the only person I have ever mentioned it to, so that must tell you something! I am an average artist of oil paintings and that is how I met Jules and his cronies. I know them well and quite a few I number as my friends. I also mix with the other side of the social scale and in some ways I have to say I have made fewer friends there than when I visit Jules! When I make friends I make firm friends, people I enjoy being with and trust.

"I studied at a number of universities in different parts of the world, and as a result I am now fluent in five languages. I say this not to boast but to explain how I can easily move from country to country just to see my friends.

"Where I have come across people struggling to look after others I have now and again set up charities to help them but without revealing my name. They give me great pleasure and my trust has never been abused; there are many good and honest people in the world, Richard."

"I wish I could share you confidence in mankind François but I have not been so lucky."

"Lucky, that's it Richard. I have been lucky all my life. I will not tell you about my failures, or my weaknesses or my appetites because overall I am both lucky and happy. Now do you think you and I can be friends and see if we can deal with this problem of yours?"

Richard looked at his new found friend and smiled.

"You are an incredible man, François. It is a privilege to know you and yes, I think we can work together!"

"Good, how much can you safely tell me, and in what way can I help?"

So Richard told him about the video tape and how Ryan had hinted that he had been approached to carry out a death threat to a well known politician; how it was earth shattering in its importance; how he had been turned down as the potential assassin and had vented his fury in front of John Vince. How Vince had been killed and then Ryan's body had been found. How the two deaths seemed to be linked, but how it was politically impossible to follow up any leads they had for danger of major political repercussions. How Ryan had been 'given' his name by Vince and that Ryan was a French-man, not an American after all.

François stayed silent trying to take it all in, then said.

"I think, Richard, that you have told me far more than your bosses would like to hear. We will share a number of confidences in the weeks to come, I have no doubt, and that is what they will always remain. I think I can fill in a number of the blanks in what you tell me but I suggest we leave it at that for now. How can I help?"

"The one avenue that may still be open to us is the grapevine of the underworld," he laughed, "How do you translate that?"

"'Telephone d'arab de la pegre'," François supplied, "You think I could find out how much the "demi-monde" knows?"

"It's a thought," said Richard, "if you would agree. In the meantime I thought you might like to see a picture of both Vince and Ryan taken off the video. That's Vince on the right, with Ryan."

The Frenchman took the photograph, examined it cursorily; then studied it again.

"Ce petit con! Je le connais!"

"You know him, François?"

"Of course, He is a crétin diablolique vraiment un homme detestable"

"Was, was. He is dead now."

*   *   *

"His name was Marcel Autriche."

"We know that," Richard confirmed, "we were told he was made redundant in 2014 when there was some form of merger. Beyond that we know very little."

"So, that is the official story, is it? What happened was the old Department, the DCRI was revamped in 2014."

"DCRI?" interrupted Richard.

"Direction Central du Renseignment Interieure. DCRI for short but more commonly known as RG. I can't remember what the RG stood for, and it doesn't matter. It was the equivalent of your MI5, dealing with internal security. They had a complete "drains up" reorganisation in 2014, and guess what? One of the more unpleasant discoveries was one Marcel Autriche. Rumours abounded at the time but the most persistent related to our friend Marcel. I gather that allegations were made linking him to bribery and corruption of the worst kind. Overnight he was out of a job; no period of notice and no pension.

My guess is that the Department could not afford the bad publicity of a prosecution so he was thrown out with no chance of compensation in exchange for a vow of silence on both sides."

"So how did you come to meet him?"

"Obviously he had contacts in the underworld and he constantly bothered them, looking for some work, either legal or illegal. You could hardly miss him – pick up the next stone and there he was!

His main difficulty was himself, whether you were a small time crook or just down-and-out, he was universally disliked. When he was in the Department, he may have been feared, even hated, but you had to listen to him and now and again deal with him because of what he represented. No longer, he now meant nothing in your life and he was made to realise it. You could almost feel sorry for him but then again, you didn't."

"Sounds a real charmer," observed Richard. "I wish I could let you listen to the tape but even if I had it I would not be allowed to."

François waved his hand dismissively.

"Of course not, I totally understand. Also I may be able to find information of use to you but I will never disclose my source and you must accept that."

"I think we understand each other, Francois."

"Of course. Now, have I got this right? You say that someone approached Autriche with a view to hiring him for an assassination attempt?"

"Yes."

"That was pretty stupid, with his reputation!"

"Well, someone did!"

"Leave it to me," said Francois, "Let's see what the grapevine has to say. Give me twenty-four hours. I will contact you here, Richard."

*   *   *

True to his word, François 'phoned Richard the next day and they arranged to meet at the hotel that evening.

"Some news," the Frenchman said, "it could be of interest. I am fairly certain I have identified someone who met with Autriche back in February but has not been seen since. It is a long shot, of course, but may be worth following up!"

"But that is over four months ago!" Richard interjected. "You would not expect someone to remember what happen-ed then, let alone be able to identify who was at a meeting with Autriche, would you?"

"Not normally, no. I agree with you but you forget what I said about Autriche's reputation and his loud mouth unpleasantness. Apparently he and this man met socially a few times and Antriche was forever boasting about how well connected and influential his friend was. Then silence. Autriche was not seen anywhere in the clubs and clubs for a number of weeks and when he did at last appear, instead of his usual obnoxious self, he was withdrawn, morose and the worse for drink. No sign of his influential friend."

"All this is pure conjecture," Richard commented.

"Perhaps, but never ignore coincidences Richard, not that you would of course in your job!" and he smiled warmly at the Englishman.

"I am really a part-time rookie, still learning on the job," he smiled back, "but it is more guesswork than proof, isn't it?"

"Of course," Richard confirmed, "but it is early days. If we can find out who this friend is then it is another part of the jigsaw, n'est ce pas? I think we will find someone who can help us but, I am afraid to say, Richard, it may need some oil to lubricate the machinery."

"You mean bribes?" Richard concluded.

"Whatever you like to call it, Richard. You must now see that we are talking about a world which is entirely foreign to you; but it is a world, that while I do not live in it, I do understand it. Information has a price; If you do not pay that price you do not get the information. Simple really."

"I may be naïve Francois, but I am not a fool! Of course I understand, but I do have to worry about where the money comes from. It is not as if the Office is averse to bribery, as long as it works, but in this particular case I am on very thin ice. I have agreed that further contact with you could well open up new lines of enquiry and I have been given a fair degree of autonomy. What I don't want to do is go back, particularly at this stage, and seek authority to spend an unknown quantity of money on bribes that might not work!"

"That, Richard, is your problem, not mine. I may be able to obtain vital information from a friendly source at no cost to me, or to Her

Majesty, but do we really think that is very likely?"

"Probably not," agreed Richard.

"Let us not fall out about it. What I will do is I will find out what I can in my own way. If that proves to be expensive, then so be it. I do not want money from you at this stage, Richard, but I would seek your personal guarantee that when it is over you will ensure I am not out of pocket. I may support or even fund charities but this is not one of them. So what's it to be?"

"You mean a personal guarantee for, theoretically, an unlimited amount irrespective of whether I can recoup it or not?"

"Trust is a difficult thing, Richard, when it comes expressed in the currency of the realm! I have told you I have trust in you, in what you stand for and your abilities. I cannot sway the decision of your Department, or Office as you so quaintly put it, but I am sure that you will be able to recover the costs, provided you can convince them that we both acted wisely and for the best, whatever the outcome."

Richard thought long and hard, balancing risks against rewards. Eventually:

"You are asking a great deal, François."

"Yes."

"I just hope I don't live to regret this! O.K. I give you my word."

"Thank you Richard, that was brave of you."

"They say fortune favours the brave. I am either being brave or a bloody idiot!"

"I wouldn't worry about it too much, Richard. I will try and keep it below €10,000."

*   *   *

Bill Smithson debriefed him in London on his return. Richard carefully played down François' involvement other than to relate the coincidence of him knowing Autriche from the past. He made no mention of possible bribes or of his personal guarantee.

"How have you left it?" Smithson asked.

"He will contact me when he has got something meaningful to report. I will need to meet him in Nice again when that happens."

127

"Oh, dear me," Smithson mocked, "do you think you will be able to manage that?"

"Someone's got to do it Bill; someone's got to do it."

CHAPTER TWENTY-ONE

"Am I not going to be invited to see your new flat, Sian?" Richard asked.

"Well you never seem to be in the country these days, let alone the village! Good of you to pop in now and again to let us know you are still alive! Just passing through, I take it, on your way to pick up your mail, then abroad again?"

"Wow! Not sure I deserved that little lecture. I was only politely asking about your flat!"

"I know, I know," smiled Sian, "but you must admit we have not seen much of you recently. I thought you had retired!"

"So did I, but you know what it's like for us celebrities; always in demand. Now am I invited round to your place or not?"

"I suppose so, as long as you behave yourself. Tomorrow afternoon? Say four pm?"

"I will be there!"

*   *   *

"I think it is very charming and very you!"

"Really? I wasn't sure at first and it did seem such a lot of money, though most of it did come from the Building Society!"

"It's all relative Sian. It's not going to lose you money, that's for sure."

"It is only one bedroom, though."

"Good, that means you can only invite people to stay if you really, really like them!"

"I know, that's what I told Tom!"

"Did you now? How did that go down?"

"I have no idea, Richard. We don't seem to be on the same wavelength these days."

"So I've heard. It happens. Anyway it is a lovely flat – hasn't Tom seen it yet?"

"No – I haven't asked him."

"Well, I think you should."

"Do you really want tea? I would have thought you were more a gin and tonic man!"

"At four pm in the afternoon? Tea would be fine, thanks Sian."

The long hot summer continues and so they had tea on the lawn as if Sian owned the panoramic view in front of them.

"Dad went to see Helen du Plessis again, when you were away, and he checked over Oliver Brady. Apparently Brady's health is deteriorating quickly – so much so that Dad is seriously considering finding him a place in a fully equipped care home. It appears that Helen's time is quickly drawing to a close. I feel sorry for her, she really has had a lot to put up with and I know she is not keen to return to South Africa."

"Have there been any repeats of the claims that he badly injured someone in his past?"

"Two or three I gather, but never in front of Dad. In that sense it is all hearsay. Let's hope it is just the ramblings of an old man."

"Maybe, but I am not so sure. I don't think we can just dismiss it but your Dad is the best judge of that; I must have a chat with him soon as I would be keen on him paying Amy Johnson another visit. Perhaps I could go with him; we'll see."

"Is that the dear old soul who used to run the Nightshelter at Winchester? I thought she had told him everything she knew."

"I am not so sure," said Richard thoughtfully, "There is something odd in that story of hers. She must have been very close to Brady to do what she did; passing on an illegal immigrant like that. It just seems strange that she then lost touch with this man who was clearly besotted with her. Anyway, that's for another time, not now. More to the point, young lady, how is your love life these days?"

"Mine?" Sian exclaimed, "It is non existent, as I told you. Unless you intend to play a part?"

"Me?" Richard burst out laughing. "Well there's a thought. I think there is only about thirty years difference between us and I have a daughter about the same age as you! Otherwise I can't see any problems at all!"

"I wasn't necessarily joking," pouted Sian. "Has it never crossed your mind?"

"If it had, I would never have told you," Richard smiled. "You pay me an enormous compliment, Sian, and I am sorry if I laughed, but it was possibly to cover up my own embarrassment. Of course I am attracted to you; what man wouldn't be? You are pretty, articulate and fun to be with. All other things on one side, though; I have made a firm friend of your father and I know full well it would just not work. I enjoy your father's company and that of his daughter and her friend and I hope very sincerely that I will be able to continue that enjoyment for a number of years yet!"

He looked across at the girl hoping that he had not upset or offended her, but he saw no tears, only a thoughtful look on a young face that gradually softened into a smile.

"Shall I take that as a 'no' then?" and the smile broadened as she spoke.

"If that is all right with you, Sian. This afternoon is mine to remember with warmth and respect. We will not allow others to share that pleasure will we?"

"Of course not," said Sian, "and thank you."

*   *   *

"I'm really not sure that is a good idea Richard"

"Look, Peter. Doesn't it seem strange to you that Amy was, it would seem, as thick as thieves with Brady at the time she was trying to persuade him to take on an illegal immigrant only to drop him like a hot cake after Freddy moves in with him?"

"Not at all Richard, why should it? As she said to me when Oliver and Freddy fell for each other, 'my presence was totally irrelevant'. It rings true to me. I am sure she was more than a little upset at the time; no woman likes to be dumped, particularly if the reason is another man! It all sounded very logical to me."

"Even to the extent of paying no interest in either Freddy or Brady and then saying she had lost touch? If she had a flaming row with Brady about Freddy and then walked out on them leaving them to their own devices. I could easily understand it, but this is not what she told you. Brady and Freddy decided to live together and all Amy does is shrug her shoulders and metaphorically wash her hands of them both and claim she had no further interest in them. Is she the sort of woman who gives in without a fight and puts them both out of her memory from that moment on? She had a close and warm relationship with Freddy, She was desperately anxious that he should be shielded from the authorities and connived with Brady to break the law. He could have shopped Amy and at any time and she knew that. Yet, according to her she did not stay in touch with either of them and could not really care less about them. Sorry, Peter, it just does not add up, not to me anyway."

"You make a strong case Richard, I'll give you that. What seems to me a logical chain of events you see as something odd, creating gaps that could be filled with what? Some evil intent on the part of a frail old lady spending her final days in a genteel care home?"

"She was not a frail old lady when all this happened," Richard pointed out. "She was a vivacious 45 year old single woman with a mind of her own!"

"I can see you are not going to let this go are you, Richard? So I will manufacture a reason to visit her again and see if I can find out anything that might fill in the gaps, satisfied?"

"Would you like me to go with you?"

"No and no again, Richard. Don't forget that I shall be visiting her as Oliver Brady's G.P., not as an undercover police agent. Thinking about it; that is more your territory isn't it? And the answer is still no!"

"Just asked , that's all"

*   *   *

"Hello, Amy. Good to see you again, looking so well too!"

"I remember you from last time Doctor Peter Jordan, you with your flattery; always the charmer!"

"Not me, Amy, I only speak the truth. You are certainly looking well and I should know!"

Amy smiled and he knew she was only half-convinced.

"I've ordered some tea for us both. At least I had some advance notice this time and am prepared for your visit. They told me you were coming."

"I thought it best to 'phone as I was not that sure you would want to see me again!"

"Why ever not? Goodness me, we have few enough visitors here and most of those are family waiting to hear that there will no longer be any need to come again and that they can inherit all the old dear's worldly goods! So, what brings you here Peter? Is it about, what was his name again? Oliver, that's it. Oliver Brady?"

"You know full well what his name is" chided Peter "and yes, Mr Brady is as well as can be expected but as I told you last time, mentally he is not doing so well which is why I wanted to see you again."

"And there I was thinking this could be the start of a little romance! Still beggars can't be choosers I suppose. I am just not sure I will be of any help Peter; it was all so many years ago."

"I know," the doctor conceded, "but the truth is, Amy, that Oliver is not going to get any better and he is in a sad place at the moment. I would do anything to take some of that sadness away and let him have some quiet enjoyment instead."

"In what way is he in a sad place?" questioned Amy, "I have been thinking about him since our last meeting and obviously if there is anyway in which I can help, I will, but it is over forty years ago!"

"I do understand, Amy, but you may be able to remember some of the past that will help me to deal with him; perhaps to allay some of his fears and worries. We all have fears or worries with which we have to cope but as one's mental strength declines they come to the surface and are difficult to deal with. You and I are lucky in that way, we still have our faculties, but poor souls like Oliver don't have that sort of strength. You did not know him for that long and maybe you can't help but if I could ask you to dig deeper?"

"Obviously something has happened with Oliver, but before you tell me about it I have been thinking about it all and reluctantly Peter, I must confess I must have misled you."

"In what way?"

"Sometimes in life, something happens and years later you regret how you dealt with it. Over time your memory almost pretends that nothing happened, but it never goes away completely; one day something brings it back to the surface.

"Maybe it's because I am reaching the end of my life, or maybe it was something you said made me think back to the past. Either way, I owe you an apology."

Peter sat in silence at this transformation from the feisty lady still challenging the world with her anecdotes and caustic observations of life to this unsure frail old lady, frightened of her own mortality.

"Amy, my love. I can't start to know where this is going, but I am no priest. I am a country doctor trying to help, if I can, one of my patients. That's all. You do not have to tell me anything if you don't want to. I do not wish to embarrass you in any way. You have nothing to apologise for."

"Tell me what has happened with Oliver that means you need to see me again?" Amy had reverted back to her inquisitive bird-like former self.

"No, Amy," the doctor said, "Tell me why you think you misled me, then we can talk about Oliver."

Momentarily Amy was confused and the uncertainty returned. She gathered her thoughts and then spoke in quiet, firm tones.

"You said Oliver was sad and that both worried and upset me. I told you that after he and Freddy got together I effectively lost touch with them both. That was not true. These days, when it seems that anything goes, the values of the past get forgotten but when Oliver and I met in 1974 they still existed. I, however, was living life to the full, and by the standards of the day I have no doubt I was categorised by some as a 'loose woman'; not that I cared. Oliver was instantly and obviously head over heels in love with me from the very start, almost embarrassingly so. I was fond of him, of course, but then I had been fond of a number of men over the years!

Oliver pursued me with an almost frightening intensity. We became lovers, he because he wanted to and me, because I didn't really mind! Isn't that shocking? I knew almost from the start that it wasn't going to last, whereas Oliver could only think of a future together. I became more and more distant and he was starting to get the message when I introduced him to Freddy.

"As I have told you before, Peter, I have never understood this 'gay' thing and I certainly did not understand it then. It would never have occurred to me that a man could be bi-sexual in that way but believe me he can! Looking back I am sure that part of his attraction to Freddy was a reaction to my increasing coolness to him.

They decided to live and love together and I, once had overcome my shock at what was happening, realised it let me off the hook. Obviously I still retained a fondness for Oliver, and Freddy had become almost like a son. I did not lose touch Peter, that is the truth. I cared deeply about them both but only from a distance."

"Why would you think you having an affair with Oliver would embarrass or shock me Amy? Those days are long gone."

"It is not that so much, it was suggesting to you that I had washed my hands of both of them once I saw them together. Anyway, let's move on! What has happened to Oliver?"

"There's probably nothing in it, but now and again he speaks some sense while most of the time he doesn't. The difficulty is knowing which is which. Recently he has been getting himself in a state, saying that he had badly hurt someone. Nothing more than that, but he is very wound up about it, whatever 'it' is! He doesn't respond when he is questioned. Most times he goes back to mumbling, but it's upsetting for him and upsetting to anyone who is there at the time. Is there anything you can recall which might give us a clue what he is talking about?"

There was no apparent reaction from Amy. She sat there, staring at Peter, who gradually felt more and more uncomfortable.

Finally:

"I'm very tired now, Doctor Jordan. It would please me if you would now leave."

CHAPTER TWENTY-TWO

The shade temperature in Nice was over thirty degrees and the streets were crowded with families determined to enjoy "les grandes vacances". Richard disliked with some intensity August in France. Paris was deserted having disgorged its population to the Cote d'Azur where prices of hotels and pensions de famille had reached astronomical levels, it was far too hot for comfort other than in air conditioned rooms and the waiters were at their rudest.

"Did you manage to find a hotel?" asked François. "With considerable difficulty," grumbled Richard. "What is it about August and the French?"

François laughed

"We call it l'instinct grégaire, the herd instinct. It is the custom in this country and it has been so for more years than I can remember, but you should let me know if you cannot find somewhere to stay; I can always find a good hotel. It is one advantage of knowing the demi-monde my friend. By the way, I am sorry you had to come all the way to Nice to see me!"

"There really is no alternative," Richard explained, "whatever the advantages of telephones, emails, texts, You-tube, Facebook and all the other 21st Century media inventions, security can never be guaranteed. Only another time, perhaps we can avoid August?"

"Bien sûr. As for now, I think you will be interested to hear what I have found out."

"As long as it doesn't mean I need a mortgage to pay for it!"

François waved his hand in a typical Gallic way.

"A mere bagatelle, my friend; It is of no importance at this stage. What is important is that I have identified the man who Marcel Autriche was praising as so important! You will remember that both he and Marcel seemed to disappear for some time and then Marcel reappears, but without this 'important' man."

"Yes, yes, I remember all that," Richard was irritated by François pedantry, "so what have you discovered?"

"One of my contacts remembers hearing Marcel boasting about this important friend of his. He called him Max in the main but on one occasion he called him Maxence."

"And?" demanded Richard.

"Max is a common enough name in France. It can be a name on its own or is more likely to be an abbreviation of a longer name, like Maximillian. But Maxence is relatively rare. It came into favour in the 1970's and to us French is considered to be an upper class name, It is certainly not a name you hear among the working classes!"

"So?" Richard was losing patience.

"Another of my contacts recognised the name Maxence. We have to assume that is the same man Marcel was boasting about, because if so, and listen to this Richard, then our own Maxence is known to be a very senior person in the DGSI – the very Department that fired Autriche in 2014!"

"So why would this Maxence want to meet a low life like Marcel," pondered the Englishman, "It doesn't make sense, does it?"

François shrugged. "It is a very odd coincidence."

"I'll say," said Richard, his excitement growing. "You have not heard the tape but I can tell you that this is becoming very political. Maybe I will have to close this line of enquiry; which will mean I will not be able to authorise you to take this any further!"

"That's probably just as well." François was totally relaxed. "I am not sure you can afford me much more!"

*   *   *

"I've had to bring '6' into the picture," Neil explained to Smithson, "we really can't have Merrington stumbling about in the south of France without telling their Office what we're up to."

It wasn't for Smithson to offer an opinion, but in his view the least said to MI6 the better. He was not convinced that Richard trod, or would tread, on their toes but these sorts of decisions were beyond his pay-grade.

"I assume that they were as mad as a hornets' nest?" was his only comment.

"Much to my surprise they seemed reasonably relaxed. I gather they have a very difficult operation going on in Paris, so all their attention is elsewhere. They even offered to examine their records to see whether this Maxence showed up on their radar!"

"And?" queried Smithson.

"Very interesting, Bill, very interesting. Reading between the lines I think they have pretty complete histories on their counterparts in France. Anyway, the point is that not only do they know about a Maxence within DGSI, they have a fairly full CV on him!"

"Wow!" Bill exclaimed, "That's impressive!"

"Or lucky," said Niel. "Either way I think it confirms that it's the same man who was meeting with Autriche. Apparently he is only a couple of rungs below the DGSI Departmental Head!"

"Things are certainly hotting up," observed Bill, "but it really is becoming political, isn't it? How on earth do we play this one now?"

"With extraordinary care, I should think. We are back to our earlier predicament; can we really avoid telling the French? I am buiggered if I am going to ask '6' for their advice! Snotty load of pin-stripes, that lot!"

"It's a bit knife-edged," admitted Smithson, "but, surely, if you tell the French, you've got to let them have the tape which in turn means bringing in the Americans. All we wanted were answers to who and why our agent was killed, not a full blown international incident which will be all over the Sun's front page before you know it!"

"Shortly to be followed by our P45's, I should think," observed Niel with some bitterness.

"It seems to me," said Bill Smiithson, choosing his words with care, "that Merrington and his side-kick, François, have played their hand rather well. You must admit, Niel, that far from blundering around in the undergrowth, they have quietly gone about their business and produced results. Not bad for beginners!"

"Even if I agreed, Bill, what's your point?"

"We all thought that it was worth a try to see if they could find some answers without clearing out the Aegean stables. Is it really such a bad idea to see if they can take it one step further?"

"And make sure that the shit doesn't fly in our direction? Nice thought, but if it goes wrong...?"

"Back to the P45's, I guess." said Bill.

*   *   *

Smithson said: "His full name is Maxence Moreau, age 45, unmarried, lives on his own in Vence, a commune between Nice and Antibes. He is one of the inter-departmental heads of the DGSI, the French security service for internal affairs.

There you are, Richard, that's your man!"

"Thank you Bill, although I am not sure what I am now going to do with the information now I have it!"

"Nor I, old boy. I think the powers that be would very much like you to fill in the gaps as it were, while they turn their backs."

"You mean I am on my own and not to go running to them if the wheels fall off?"

"That's the ticket, Richard, got it in one! You know the score as well as I do. Their biggest worry is your mate François. He seems to have been a safe pair of hands so far, but let's face it, he is not one of us, he is even French, for God's sake, and you are putting a lot of faith in him and upstairs are feeling uncomfortable. Thing is they have three options: One; call off the whole investigation and just file it away. Two; disclose our hand to both the French and Americans, stand back and watch the fire-works or three; see what you can come up with, with your dubious underground dealings."

"Do thank them for their vote of confidence won't you?" Richard said sarcastically. "As to François what is the real difference between my situation not that long ago and François now? If you recall I was called in to help occasionally and for certain someone was taking a chance on me. Same with François. I trust him but if you can't accept that I will also step down. Your decision. Just let me know in due course won't you?"

"Now don't go all girlish on me Richard Merrington," admonished Bill. "They are giving you a vote of confidence by including you in the options. And I think they are right to be concerned about François. It means you have to be doubly careful about what you tell him and how far you take this. Getting it wrong is not an option, Richard.

For example, I assume you have not told him anything but the basics about the tape? Have you mentioned the Americans?"

"Of course not Bill. Now you are getting me cross. All he knows is that Vince met a man in a bar who talked to him about a political killing and he had not been given the job. François identified Autriche and he has now discovered that Autriche was first approached by Maxence. End of story. Satisfied?"

"If you are satisfied Richard, then so am I. I think the problem will be from now on. We can confirm that Maxence is leading figure in the DGSI. Of course you will have to tell François and how will he take it? Won't he want to defend his equivalent of MI5? And won't there be a conflict of interest?"

"When Burgess and Blunt were both outed as being Russian spies within MI6 did everyone think that their own security systems were rotten to the core or that there were some bad apples that had to be rooted out? Same difference."

"No, not quite, but let's not go there. You understand my general point though? It is going to be very tricky for you and the stakes are very high. Do you really want to do this?"

"I probably understand more than you think Bill. I will be devastated if the trust between me and François is broken and I am totally aware of the political consequences. What else can I say? Yes, Bill, I really want to do this."

"I guessed that would be your answer, Richard, and I wish you all the luck in the world. Oh, there is one further thing you should know."

"Yes?"

"You remember I told you that '6' have somehow obtained Maxence's file which included his C.V. Nothing particularly remarkable in any of it other than one entry which we have translated. "In 2012 Maxence was summoned to an internal enquiry 'To investigate the relationship of the employee' (that is Maxence, Bill explained) 'with an employee of Marchandises S.A, contrary to the terms of employment of the Division. Case dismissed for lack of evidence; Caution issued.' We are reliably informed that Marchandises S.A is effectively the registered office through which the Central Intelligence Agency operates". Thought you should know Richard!"

CHAPTER TWENTY-THREE

"Richard won't be back for a while. He thinks it could be two weeks or even more to sort out the business problems he has."

Sian snorted "he must have a secret mistress over there! Come to think of it considering how much time he spends in the south of France he must have a string of bordellos!"

"Quite possibly Sian," Peter was not in the mood for scurrilous gossip. "I mention it," he said, "because we should agree on the next steps on the Headstone issue; now that I have had the second meeting with Amy, I don't think we can wait for Richard to come back, bit I think the three of us, you Sian, Tom and I need to work out a plan of action. Can you gather up Tom, Sian, or are you two still not talking?"

"Oh, we're o.k. Dad," Sian smiled. "I just wish he would grow up a bit!"

"And he probably wishes you weren't so condescending. He is a good few years younger than you Sian and has not experienced life much outside this village. Give him a break, he is not a bad lad and he is nobody's fool."

"I know. Perhaps we can persuade Richard next time to take Tom with him on his travels; That should get him out and about and give him a bit of worldly experience!"

"What, and get Richard to take Tom to all these bordellos you were talking about? That would certainly make him or break him!"

"I'll tell you what Dad, let's have the meeting at my flat. Tom has never been there and I would quite like to show it to him."

"Fine by me; you set it up Sian."

*　　*　　*

"Now we've had the grand tour, can we get on and talk about Amy Johnson?" Peter asked.

"It is a very nice flat, Sian," said Tom.

"Thank you."

"Just don't mention it only has one bedroom, eh Sian?" said her father, "Now, I have told you about my latest meeting with Amy; so what conclusions do we reach?"

Tom's reaction was both immediate and decisive.

"Do we believe anything she tells us? She has obviously lied extensively in the past and we should question both her motives and the truth of what she is now saying. I am not sure I buy this fear of mortality as a reason for a sudden change of heart. You've met her Peter, and this all has a false ring to it. Well it does to me anyway."

"I know what you mean Tom," said Sian, "but it seems to me that Amy has always led a life of extremes. She may be making all this up but I think it is unlikely; what particularly intrigues me is her reaction, or rather lack of it, to your comment about Oliver living in the past. If she had been living a life of lies then surely she would have clammed up and sent you packing Dad?"

"You both make good points and I think the answer lies somewhere in between. Firstly I do not believe that the Amy I first met; the lively, witty. bright eyed, always ready with a quip sharp as a button Amy, is the real Amy anymore than the latest edition of her being a frail, old soul ready to confess her sins for fear of retribution in the hereafter! I sense that she did have an affair with Oliver and that she did lose touch with him or with Freddy, but her reaction when she blanked me at the end of our conversation convinces me she was not going to tell me the truth, the whole truth and nothing but the truth!"

"The trouble is," said Tom, "that she has told you enough to whet your appetite, and ours too, come to that, but we have no idea where this is leading us. It sounds as though it is only Amy who can fill in the gaps but your chances of arranging another meeting don't seem great!"

"No," Peter admitted, "and at the moment I can see no legitimate reason to ask for another meeting; if she does not want to talk to me than that is her prerogative. Let's call it off for now and meet up at the weekend at my place, perhaps one of us will have had a brainwave by then."

"And perhaps not," said Sian gloomily

*   *   *

"Could I speak with Dr Peter Jordan please?"

"Speaking."

"Oh good. Dr Jordan, I am the duty manager at the Brushwood Care Home. You were kind enough to leave your contact details with us the last time you visited Amy Johnson. Am I right in thinking you are not Miss Johnson's GP? Only she was confused about that."

"No, I am certainly not; I am a medical doctor but one of my patients is an old friend of Amy's and I was hoping she could give me a little background on him; how can I help?"

"She was very anxious that we should contact you. I am afraid she is not too well at the moment; although as you are a GP I am sure I can go into a little bit more detail. She has been seen by the doctor who is on call for our emergencies, a Dr Strong. We are only a care home; we do not provide medical services here. Amy had not been her usual self and we were concerned enough to ask for her to be examined. Apparently she has had a series of mini-strokes. At this stage we are told there is no immediate need for her to go to hospital and that the best thing is for her to rest. The doctor will examine her again to-morrow and we then decide where we go from there."

"I am very sorry to hear that," said Peter. "How can I help?"

"Amy is very anxious to see you, apparently. I know no more than that but she says she must see you as soon as possible. All I have done is promise to contact you so I am happy that I have managed to do so."

"Well, thank you for your call. I do appreciate it, but I don't think she should be thinking about having visitors just yet. That is a decision for Dr Strong and certainly not one for Amy to make. Of course I will see her again if she wishes but only when her doctor says so. Would you mind explaining that to her?"

"Of course. Perhaps you could give me a ring, in say two days time? We should know more by then."

*   *   *

"Hello, Amy my love. Someone told me you were not feeling too well but I must say you look fighting fit to me!"

"Oh, I'm all right, Peter, doctors fuss too much! I felt a bit wobbly once or twice but I am fine now. I am not prepared to pack my bags quite yet and I did want to talk to you. We have some unfinished business, you and I!"

"So I believe. Although I thought you had seen enough of me last time?"

"Stuff and nonsense. That was last time and I was tired. Now is now and I am not tired! So where were we?"

"Amy, do be sensible. I am quite sure Dr Strong told you to rest quietly and avoid too much excitement. Are you sure you want to do this?"

"I will tell you what I don't want. I don't want to be comatose like most of the others you see here. Life is for living; there is plenty of time for dying and it's not yet!"

"I am fairly certain the good Lord above would not want to contradict you Amy; anymore than I would. Just take it carefully, that's all!"

"I have reached a decision Peter. Believe it or not I may not have much time left and I want to get this business of Olly and Freddy out of the way while I can."

"Only if you really want to Amy."

"Yes, I do. I have been keeping this secret for too long now. From what you tell me anything I say will no longer hurt Oliver and as for Freddy," she spread her hands out wide, "who knows and does it really matter?"

"Tell me Amy," Peter's curiosity drove him to ask, "do you know Freddy's real name?"

"Of course I do. Always have but it can't hurt him now. His Polish name is, or probably was, Frederyck Karolek." Amy spelt it out so that the doctor could write it down. "That's why we called him Freddy Carol; at least he could remember that easily enough. We did everything we could to keep his identity a secret. We were both terrified that he would be traced as an illegal immigrant and deported or even jailed!"

"Did Oliver know his full name?"

"Not sure, probably, why do you ask?"

"I will come to that in a while, Amy. So you saw Oliver regularly, I take it?"

"From time to time. He was not living where he is now, of course. Occasionally we would meet up in a pub some way outside the village. He was almost paranoiac about keeping the secret of Freddy living with him, which I respected, although I could never fully understand. It was nobody else's business but you would be hard pushed to keep a secret like that for long in a country village!"

"I had not realised that he used to live somewhere else other than his present flat. Was that in the village?"

"A little way outside. It was a large Victorian style house with four or even five bedrooms; far too big for him of course. It would have been about a mile or so from XL Solutions; he always said that he would never bring his work back to his home nor take his personal life to work. It was a pleasant enough house with a lovely garden which he looked after and he stayed there until he started to fall ill and was retired from the firm."

"When was that, Amy?"

"Sometime in 1994 I think, or maybe a year later. I think the house has since been demolished and replaced with a Regency style building with porticos and all the trimmings. Haven't seen it, but so I am told."

"And Freddy was living with him all that time?"

"Until Oliver retired, yes. To be truthful I did not see much of Freddy during that time as, although I was very fond of him in the earlier years, he gradually changed for the worse."

"In what way?"

"Oh, I don't know exactly. He seemed to be less open and said some unpleasant things about Olly; I could not easily forgive that. Oliver had taken him in under his wing; provided a home for him; gave him expenses and would do anything for him. To me it seems a bit strange to talk about Oliver loving another man, but I think he did over all those years and he was hurt by some of the things Freddy said."

"You had no problems with the authorities?"

"As it happens, no. Mainly because he was under Olly's wing I suppose. Freddy had no reason to sign on with the authorities, no need to claim any benefits, no need for a passport. To the world at large he just did not exist. Luckily he must have been very healthy; as far as I know he had no need for a doctor or a hospital. Oliver looked after him, cared for him and paid for him in every way, which is why those nasty traits in Freddy's character upset me so much."

"Yes, I am sure they did. What were the disagreements about? Why the nasty comments?"

"I think that as time went on and the early flush of romance died away Freddy became more and more unsettled. Oliver told me he had started asking questions as to why he was unregistered and how he wanted to live a proper life and why wouldn't Olly sort things out with the authorities? He did not seem to realise that Olly and I could be in serious trouble if the truth came out; he was only thinking about himself."

"Amy, I must leave you now. I had promised Dr Strong that I would not overstay my welcome and he was insistent I only stayed for ten minutes or so and I have already over-run!"

"You will come again though, Peter, won't you? There is a lot more I want to tell you and it makes me feel so much better to talk about it all. Purging of the soul or something like that, I suppose!"

"You and I will both do what we are told by Dr Strong, Amy. I will certainly be back as soon as I can."

"And, Peter, please assure me that Olly can come to no harm now, now that he is so ill."

"I have no idea what you still have to tell me and I do not have that sort of authority. What I will say is the there are plenty of cases where the onset of dementia in its more severe form have meant the Crown Prosecution Service has not proceeded with its enquiries, and from what you have told me so far, I do not think there is any reason whatsoever for the CPR to investigate anything."

"Maybe not so far, Peter, but I still have more to tell you!"

"Maybe, Amy, but not now. We will talk soon, very soon I hope."

"I hope so, I really do hope so" said Amy.

*   *   *

"So how do you assess Amy now?" Tom asked. "You will remember that I thought we could not believe a word she said!"

"I am quite aware of that, Tom," answered Peter, "and even I wasn't sure how much we could trust her to tell the truth. I think what has changed though is her recent illness. She still has that air of bravado about her but underneath it all I think she is a frightened old lady. She has come face to face with mortality and she knows she has lived too long with the Olly/Freddy charade. She is not a religious lady, so there is no priest to confess to and it is surprising how often terminally ill patients want to tell all to their doctors. So, yes, up to now I believe what she has told me. Goodness knows what comes next!"

"Is she terminally ill then?" Sian asked her father.

"Not medically speaking, no she is not. But a mini-stroke, or, as in this case, a series of mini-strokes, mean that a severe stroke is a real possibility and could well result in death. Bear in mind her age and her chances don't look that good, and I sense she knows that."

"Poor old soul," sympathised Sian, "what she must have gone through all these years!"

"As ye sow, so shall ye reap" said Tom.

CHAPTER TWENTY-FOUR

"François," said Richard, "things are getting a little tricky, I am afraid to say!"

"In what way?"

"We have unearthed information about Maxence which, to put it mildly, is highly confidential; I cannot decide what to do with it."

"I see," said François cautiously, "is this a case of 'FOR YOUR EYES ONLY' meaning you, and not me?"

"As always, François, you are one jump ahead of me. I cannot decide whether to ignore the rules and tell you what I've been told, even though that means I break my word and breach confidences. On the other hand if I don't tell you then I can't see how we can move forward."

"It would seem to me you are damned if you do and damned if you don't!" Francois observed. "Rather you than me."

"Thanks for that, Francois. That really is a great help!"

"Yes, sorry about that. Let's tackle this logically. If you decide that you can't tell me, which I would totally understand, then it seems to me that our part of the operation has to come to an immediate halt. Your people would then have to decide what to do next but for certain you would not be part of their plans. Are you all right with that?"

"I have to be. This is not a personal glory mission; nor should it be. To be honest it would almost be a relief. On the other hand I would be disappointed."

"Of course you would, I understand that. Look Richard, I am the problem: I can see that. Here I am, the outsider with a curious set of friends, some no doubt with criminal records, a Frenchman to boot, offering to use his knowledge of the murky part of this society to help you, an Englishman, find out who took out your agent in cold blood on the soil of my country.

"It's relatively easy, some would say, to forget all about Vince's death. After all it could be argued that this was just one more casualty in this dirty trade! It happened, time passes and we may even forget the name of the agent who was killed, or why, and should anyone really care?

"That's just not our style, Richard. We can't just walk away from this but if you feel you cannot tell me that's what we will be doing. As I have said before it's all a question of trust and I know you trust me. But before you come to a decision you must never forget that we are all humans, both of us. I hope you continue to show trust in me and I will honour that as far as humanly possible but the real risk you would run is if I made a mistake, or said something which I should not have said; not because I am reckless but because I am human. You cannot guard against that, Richard, and you must include that factor in reaching your decision."

Richard had sat quietly while his friend was speaking, admiring the intrinsic honesty of the man; knowing he could trust him even as he identified the quandary in which Richard now found himself.

"Thank you," he said simply. "I think the risks for me are far less than the ones you may face in the future, assuming you are happy to carry on working with me?"

"Yes Richard, I am. To set the record straight, I am not interested in money. I have more than enough as it is and my life was becoming a little pointless. I have just as much interest as you in seeing justice done, if that is at all possible. It gives us both a goal to aim for, but we are very different people you and I. Absolute honesty between us will overcome any difficulties that would otherwise intrude. Did you know for example that I do not smoke or do drugs – but I do drink – sometimes too much – gamble and sleep with pretty women whenever possible?"

"I think I could have guessed all of those, François, particularly the last. You are after all a Frenchman."

"And you Richard, are an Englishman, You are courteous and fair and honest. You are also, how you say, 'bloody-minded', occasionally irritating and lacking in imagination. You probably don't gamble but I think you could drink and sleep around given the chance, if only your English reserve would let you. Is that a fair assessment?"

"As a very English character once said, 'You may think that, but I could not possibly comment!'"

*   *   *

"Some of what I tell you, François, is fact and some of it is deduction and theory. I will not say which is which; you can guess if you want but for our purposes it makes no difference. You were the first to identify Maxence; as you said a leading figure in the DGSI. Our people already know him; know quite a lot about him in fact. Maxence Moreau is a departmental head and one of his staff with whom he was particularly friendly was indeed Marcel Autriche, otherwise known to our John Vince as Ryan. Maxence fought very hard to keep Autriche when it was decided in 2014 to get rid of him and probably persuaded his boss to avoid any bad publicity. We think he kept unofficial contact with Autriche after he was sacked and the guess is that Maxence had benefited in the past from Autriche's contacts in the underworld and he was desperate to keep the relationship going.

If the theory is right Maxence was contacted by some unknown person offering a great deal of money if Maxence could arrange for the assass-ination of a major political figure."

François interrupted "I assume you know the name of this politic-ian?"

"Yes," Richard admitted, "I was hoping to avoid telling you!"

"Understood. I will assume that this would be in Paris in the middle of summer. Do continue, Richard, – no wait. So Maxence contacted Autriche. That would make sense as they had been friends and now Autriche was out of work but still valuable to Maxence, I think I under-stand."

"Also, that would have been a convenient arrange-ment for Maxence," explained Richard, "If it went to plan then he could claim he knew nothing about it and would be able to pay Autriche enough to ensure his silence. Always assuming he lived to tell the tale, of course. If it went wrong Maxence would have had little difficulty in having Autriche taken out."

"Which is precisely what happened, as I see it," concluded François.

"We assume so. We have no proof of course. Indeed we have no positive proof that it was Maxence from the DGSI. It could have been some other Maxence, for all we know!"

"Yes, Richard. How do you say – pigs might fly?"

"Quite. But you see how political this is becoming? This could bring down the French government!"

"I doubt it Richard. In England if a Cabinet Minister is found having rude sex with his mistress, then the British government may well collapse. In France the Minister would be applauded."

*   *   *

"Richard, we need to meet!" Smithson hated having to make contact by mobile 'phone, fully aware that it could be intercepted. He was trained to make the calls as brief as possible so that any interception would be valueless but he could never control what might be said in reply.

"If you say so," said Richard, "but I am not at home at the moment. Can it wait? I should be home by the weekend."

It was not what Smithson wanted. Merrington had agreed to attend the de-briefing sessions every week, such was the Office's sensitivity to Richard's lack of field experience and his association with the Frenchman. Two weeks had now gone by and all that Smithson knew was that Merrington was in France and obviously had every intention of staying there, at least in the short term. He knew that as things stood he was powerless, which did not improve his mood.

"Do try and make the meeting on Monday then!" was the best he could think of at that moment.

*   *   *

"The next step, it seems to me," said François, "is to find out who it was that contacted Maxence about the assassination."

"I am not sure how we do that," Richard replied, "even with your connections I don't see how we can find out if Maxence won't tell us!"

"I was not suggesting we ask him!" François' sarcasm was thinly hidden, "have you any better ideas?"

"Probably. If all our theories, or guesses if you like, are correct than the first step is surely to analyse who killed Autriche and on whose orders. Can we start there?"

"You mean, can I start there?" queried François, seemingly annoyed, "I could ask around I suppose, but it could be dangerous."

"I do realise that François," Richard tried to be conciliatory, "but we have to start somewhere!"

"Agreed!" François said, suddenly positive. "It seemed that our proposed 'entente cordiale' was in danger of not being so 'cordiale', my friend!"

"I do know what you mean. Shall we call it a draw?"

"Certainment, mon ami. We really must grow up, I think. I will start straight away and report back, O.K?"

"O.K., and good luck!"

*   *   *

"Well done so far," Smithson said, "but do we have to use this François? Everyone is very twitchy about that!"

"Bill, I have gone over this countless times. I totally trust the man, as you know, but that apart how do you suggest we pick up the underground grapevine without him? And his full name is François Duval, should it be of interest. I am getting a little tired of all this. For the last time, let me get on with the job! If I want to use Duval then I will. Either that or we stop right here and I will go back home to the uncomplicated pastures of Hampshire!"

"O.K Richard. I have got the message. Indeed I had it at the last meeting if you recall. I am just as pissed off as you are but the powers that be are like cats on a hot tin roof and as you are seldom here I get all the pressure. It is agreed to let you play this your way but you have three weeks to wrap it up!"

"What!"

"Loud and clear Richard, loud and clear. If you have not got it all sorted in three weeks you are off the case and we close it down. It is non-negotiable. That is the message from on high, and I mean on high!"

"Sometimes, Bill," said Richard, "you can be an absolute shit!"

CHAPTER TWENTY-FIVE

"I have been talking to Dr Strong," Peter told Sian. "you remember he was the G.P attending to Amy. Anyway, not good news, I am afraid. Apparently she has had yet another mini-stroke and Strong has insisted she is transferred to the main hospital in Winchester to be kept under close observation."

"Is she already there? Does it mean she is a lot worse?" Sian felt concern for Amy although she had not met her.

"Not as such," Peter explained "It is more that, medically speaking, the greater the frequency of strokes the greater the risk of major trauma, The care home could not even start to look after her then. Strong says she is still asking after me which makes it all very difficult. In one sense there is no reason why I should not pay her a short visit, particularly as she will get more agitated until I do. On the other hand stress should be avoided at all costs, for fear of the consequences'. I will have to go, I think. Strong agrees with me and will be giving her a mild sedative. Not a happy visit though."

"No," agreed Sian, "It is not the end of the world, Dad, if we call an end to all our enquiries. It is certainly not worth putting her life at risk, that is for sure!"

"If only it was as simple as that! If I don't go she will get increasingly more stressed. If I do go she will get stressed just by reliving the past. Wish me luck Sian!"

"More to the point. I wish Amy luck!" said Sian fervently.

*　　*　　*

"Now what have you been getting up to Amy?"

Amy smiled, but it was a weak smile, a smile of resignation.

"I can't beat the system, Peter, as well you know. The one thing I always said was that I would spend my last days in my own bed in my own home. Now look at me!"

"You can still make your ambition Amy; just do what you are told, get better and stuff the system!"

Amy laughed.

"If only," she said, "but I shall try my best. I shall be a lot happier if I can tell the truth and shame the devil. Now where were we?"

"Amy, listen to me. What matters now is for you to get better: it may be that by telling me what happened with Olly and Freddy you will be able to lighten up, but there will be a cost to pay. By telling me you will bring back memories that you have for years shut away in a dark cupboard and almost forgotten. Are they best not left there? Do you really want to open the door and see these memories flooding back, just to create stress and worry that you have successfully dealt with for years?"

Amy, for her, was unusually quiet and when she spoke it was in a measured, almost unemotional, tone.

"You are a good man, Doctor Peter," she said, "and you mean well. But what you don't know is the turmoil that I have lived with all these years and the price that I have already paid. In one sense I am sorry for you, Peter, as you should by curious chance be the conduit for my emotions, my release valve, if you like. Do remember, Peter, that:-

'All the world is a stage. And
all the men and women are merely players.
They have their exits and their entrance,
and one man in his time plays many parts.'

So there we are Peter – it is time to play one's part don't you think?"

It was Peter's turn to fall quiet. He looked at this now frail old lady who had challenged the world head on all her life and now needed to let the memories flood back.

"I think recounting it all is what you want, Amy, and I admire you for it, but if it hurts too much hide the truth and I will understand and respect that."

"I know you will. Where were we up to? "

"Freddy was starting to have rows with Oliver about wanting to be registered, to lead a more normal life."

"Oh, yes. By then he and Olly had been together about ten years, and the idea of disclosing everything to the authorities horrified both of us. We had no idea what our legal position would be and had no wish to find out! Olly was stressed beyond belief as the atmosphere between them got worse and worse and looking back that could have been the start of Olly's illness."

"Surely though, Freddy was allowed out of the house from time to time?" questioned Peter.

"At first, yes, once Olly had explained to Freddy why it was necessary for the three of us to prevent anyone from finding out the truth. So Freddy willingly concocted some fictional story to tell people how he had come to live in England, his current job, how long he could stay in the country and how he went home to visit relatives he had left in Poland. At the start Freddy thought it was a huge joke and was more than happy to go along with the deception. But of course the joke stopped being so funny and when Freddy started being nasty about being registered the rows started. Olly tried, mostly successfully, to stop Freddy going out and the tensions dramatically increased. It was about that time that my mother, who lived in the Midlands, became critically ill and I ended up staying there for weeks at a time until she eventually died. So I did not see or hear anything about the dramas occurring and when I did it was too late to save the situation. And then…" and her voice trailed off.

Peter waited for her to regain her composure but she was desperately trying to hold back the tears.

"Shall we leave it there Amy?"

"No, I am all right. It is as you said it might be, painful to remember. It hurts more than I would have thought!" and she smiled through her tears at the doctor.

"Amy, you must stop; this is too stressful!"

"No Peter, don't you see. It is the stress of all those years starting to be released. Don't be alarmed. I really I am a tough old bird!"

"What happened, Amy? What happened after you came back from your mothers?"

"I had a 'phone call from Olly. I had never heard him crying before and I never want to hear it again. He was sobbing his heart out and in between sobs he was saying over and over again 'Help me Amy, help me! There is blood everywhere!'"

She paused and gathered her strength to continue.

"I had no idea what had happened, Peter, no idea! I didn't know who had been hurt! All I knew was I had to get there. I remember getting in my car but I can't remember driving there. My mind was all over the place and images flashed through my mind. Secretly I still loved Olly, despite everything that had happened and I was both scared and emotional, having no idea what I was to find."

Peter knew she was not to be interrupted and he wanted her to re-group before she continued.

"I cannot describe what I saw when I got there, partly because I don't want to but also because the memories are almost subliminal. They are like a sequence of pictures flashed on a screen, one following another almost too quickly to take them all in. All I know is Freddy was shouting with his right hand clasped to his left shoulder and blood still being forced out between his fingers. In a corner of the room sat Olly, his face a horrible parchment colour, with tears streaming down his face and on the floor was either a bread knife, or a carving knife, lying in a pool of blood. There was blood everywhere, or so it seemed!"

"Amy, that's terrible!" Peter was genuinely aghast at what he had heard. "What did you do?"

"In my early years I was a nurse, a fully qualified SRN believe it or not, so I knew what to do. Neither of the two of them was capable of doing anything. Olly was in total shock and Freddy could not stop staring at his shoulder. I think it was the sight of his own blood more than anything else; he was in severe shock and close to passing out. What they would have done if I had not turned up I do not know.

"I concentrated on Freddy; at that stage there was little I could do to help Olly. I made Freddy take his hand away from his shoulder so that I could at least examine the wound but first I had to cut away the shirt with some scissors I found in the kitchen. Luckily the wound was not as bad as I first thought. The knife had penetrated the chest wall close to the armpit and had also lacerated his arm but no major artery seemed to be severed, at least not in the arm itself. Most of the blood came from skin lacerations to the arm; while the point where the blade had entered the chest cavity was almost closed, with blood oozing from the puncture.

"I then made Olly useful by boiling some water and finding some clean linen and then by making strong tea for the three of us, with plenty of sugar for the shock.

In the bathroom I found a first-aid cabinet which by sheer luck contained unopened packets of sterilized bandages which I used to place over the puncture and the worst of the arm wounds.

"I wanted to call for an ambulance but both Olly and Freddy were vehemently opposed to that idea, probably because of fear of involving any authorities. Very reluctantly I gave in and persuaded them to take to their beds and try to sleep which, surprisingly, they agreed to.

"By now I was satisfied that the injuries were not life threatening, so I agreed to come back in the morning. The next day, having looked at Freddy's injuries I became uneasy. There were signs of the wounds turning septic and I pleaded with them to allow me to take Freddy to A & E. They would have none of it. When I had Freddy on his own I asked him what had happened but he refused to talk, no matter how much I begged.

"I then tackled Olly, while Freddy was in the kitchen. He broke down again but between his tears told me that Freddy had started yet another row and this time things got so heated that Freddy grabbed hold of the bread-knife and threatened him. They wrestled, Freddy slipped and fell to the floor impaling himself with the knife as he did so."

"Did you believe that's what happened Amy?"

"This was the man I had secretly loved all those years. Of course I wanted to believe him, so as Freddy refused to answer my questions, I did."

"Do you now?"

"Same answer Peter. Anyway, Olly said that he had to attend a critical meeting at XL Solutions that afternoon and that we should see how things were the next day. So I went to work, full of misgivings. The next thing was a 'phone call from Olly at about eight o'clock. He had returned home to find the house empty but ransacked from top to bottom and a cash box that Olly kept in a desk drawer taken and the contents of £500 gone. There was no note from Freddy and he did not return. I don't mean that night – I mean ever. Neither of us have seen Freddy from that day to this."

Peter was rendered virtually speechless. He sat in the visitors' chair in Amy's hospital room, unable to think of anything to say that would have stemmed the tears that were now flowing down the old lady's cheeks. So many questions still to be asked. So many loose ends to be gathered up, and yet he knew it was not the time.

"Thank you Amy, my love," was all he could bring himself to say as he got up from his chair, "perhaps we could talk again sometime, though not now."

"I understand, Peter, and I am now really rather tired. Next time I will answer all the questions you must still have for me. I am so glad to have told you."

Three days later Amy Johnson had a hemorrhagic stroke and died at the hospital.

*   *   *

"I feel awful," said Sian, "that poor woman and everything she has been through, to end like that!"

"Obviously it is a sad time," Tom agreed, "but I come back to the point I made the other day. She lied her way into that situation; when you think back it all started when she covered up the fact that Freddy was an illegal immigrant. From that moment on it all went downhill and inevitably ended in tragedy."

Peter could see Sian's blood pressure had risen exponentially as Tom was talking and knew he should intervene.

"Hold on a moment Tom. You seem to forget that Olly and Freddy shared a happy life together for a number of years! Anyway the truth seems to be that that there is nothing more we can, or indeed, should do now that Amy has died. Oliver is way beyond being of any rational help to us. Freddy apparently disappeared off the face of the earth. He may easily be dead by now, even if he recovered from his injuries and always assuming Oliver did not kill him, which I think remains a distinct possibility. We will never know and I can't see there is any point in bringing in the authorities in any way whatsoever. Let Amy die in peace and leave Oliver alone with whatever memories he has, good or bad."

"And leave the story of Freddy out there, still unsolved with nobody knowing whether he lived or died or even caring? Surely that can't be right?" Sian's frustration was self-evident. Then she deliberately took the perilous task of tackling her own father.

"Don't you think, Dad, that Amy's illness and her death were due to you questioning her so aggressively?"

In an instant the atmosphere became super-charged only to be broken by Tom.

"I think you should withdraw that statement Sian. To my mind it was both thoughtless and unfair!"

"No, Tom," said Peter, "let's deal with this now that it is on the table. I probably agree with Tom, Sian, that you have put the question with insufficient thought. It was an emotional question, not a logical one."

He raised his hand to stop his daughter rising to the bait.

"Just listen to me for a moment. Do you think we doctors are never attacked by distressed relatives who need to hit out in their own grief? Do you think we don't go over and over again, in our own minds, whether we could have avoided the final outcome? And do you believe that we never ever make mistakes that we have to live with? Not clinical mistakes: I am not talking about that. I am talking about mistakes of nuance, seeing atmospheres and not dealing well with them, failing to anticipate the consequences of well meaning or thoughtless words or actions. Believe me Sian, I have been there many times!"

"Let's all move on," said Tom. "I suggest we sift through all the information we have gathered and what questions remain unanswered, I think I agree with you Peter. I doubt very much that we are going to find many more answers, but you never know, we might have missed something."

"Hold on a minute, you two!" said Peter, "that's my 'phone in the other room. I won't be a moment!"

When they were alone Tom took Sian's hand.

"Are you all right now? Sorry I said what I did, or at least the way I said it!"

"No, it's O.K. Tom. You were both quite right, of course. I wish we had never started on this stupid enquiry and just left everything alone. What, in all honesty, have we really achieved? I feel uncomfortable about the whole thing!"

Tom gave a half-laugh.

"Well, blame Richard for that. If only he had not seen the headstone! Talking of which nobody has ever mentioned the headstone, as far as I can remember. Yet another unanswered question!"

Peter was glad to see then sitting together when he returned. He had a cordial dislike of atmospheres.

"Well, would you believe it? Most extraordinary! That was Winchester Hospital. Apparently Amy spent the last two days of her life on earth writing me a long letter. It is there waiting for me to collect it!"

CHAPTER TWENTY-SIX

"Three weeks! You are not serious Richard?"

"I have never been more serious, François. Either we have all the answers in three weeks or I am off the case and that I am afraid would include you!"

"C'est incroyable! Why only three weeks? What is so special about three weeks? Incroyable!"

"I know, but there is nothing I can do to change it. Twenty one days is our limit, so we had better plan very carefully. Are you still up for it?"

"Of course. Let me find out what I can about Maxence and his movements. Perhaps we can have a nice friendly conversation with him soon?"

"He lives in Vence but works here in Nice," Richard said. "Beyond that we have no useful information."

"It's not what you know, it's who you know. Leave that to me, Richard. We shall meet again tomorrow at noon, yes?"

"Yes, I shall have drawn up a list of priorities for each of us by then."

*   *   *

"This is not going to work, my friend, You are not telling me the whole truth about Maxence are you?"

"I'm not with you, in what way?" asked Richard.

"I have a contact who has met Maxence at a cocktail party. Maxence is an arrogant 'salaud' who talks in a loud voice about himself. After he had moved on, someone standing nearby said 'il s'en sortit de justesse', meaning that Maxence was lucky to still have a job, mentioning an internal enquiry a few years ago into his association with someone from the CIA. Now don't tell me, Richard, that you did not know about this? You boasted you had practically seen his C.V.!"

It was a dangerous moment and Richard knew it. He had agreed with London that he would not tell François of the American connection.

"It was my decision not to tell you," he explained. "naively I suppose, I thought we could identify who killed both Autriche and Vince without bringing in the possible CIA link. That way you would not be exposed to the wider political scene and the risks involved. I was wrong and I am sorry."

"Fine words, Richard, but then you are very clever with your words. I can see now why you are rated so highly by your superiors. In your dirty world of espion-age I assume there is no room for honesty, which is a pity because I relied on the trust between us."

"That may be a little harsh," Richard replied, wanting to lower the temperature between them. "Maybe I was wrong to do so but I was, in a clumsy way, trying to keep you out of unnecessary trouble."

"Really?" François sounded unconvinced. "I think I will sleep on it Richard. I am far from certain I wish to carry on with this!"

*   *   *

They would normally meet at the corner café on the fringes of the market in the old town. In the summer months they sat outside in the warmth of the early morning sun with croissants and cafes Americains, along with locals and a few tourists who preferred its atmosphere and informality.

He was not certain if or when François might appear, so he bought a Nice-Matin from the tabac a few doors away and improved his French vocabulary as he read. It was suitably noisy where they sat which guaranteed safety of their confidences when the two of them did meet.

"I am pleased that you are not reading The Daily Telegraph," said François as he sat down alongside Richard. "At least you have good taste!"

"I can't afford the price of imported papers," explained Richard, with a smile, "otherwise I would. Bonjour, François, ça va?"

"Your accent does not improve either" chided the Frenchman, "just as well you are going home soon!"

"Not for three weeks, I hope. I am very pleased to see you, my friend!"

"Yes, well yesterday has gone and we can start afresh today. I am still not sure that you deserve it but I will overlook it this once. Do not ever do that again!"

"Je fais mes excuses humiliantes, Monseigneur!"

"Not sure that grovelling suits you, my friend. However, enough of this crap. You get me a coffee and croissant while I read your Nice-Matin. Sounds fair enough to me!" and his grin showed that this particular storm had passed.

*   *   *

"Like it or not, Richard, and in all seriousness you realise, I hope, that I can now fathom out most, if not all, of the politics involved?"

"Of course, and I will have to answer for that in due course. There is nothing to be gained in my packing my bags and going back to the office with my tail between my legs so, for what it is worth, my proposal is that we move on at the best possible speed and see if we can solve this riddle in three weeks."

"Less two days, so far," reminded François. "I think we can make an intelligent guess at what happened and why although I am not sure that we can be certain who was responsible for what!"

"I agree," said Richard. "Let's got through what we know and where it leads us."

Richard had already decided that, as he put it to himself, 'he may as well be hung for a sheep rather than a lamb' and there was nothing to be gained in not telling François the whole story as he knew it. As they talked Richard realised the Frenchman had already worked out, or at least had guessed at, the existence and extent of the American involvement. So between them they put the pieces of the jigsaw together, where necessary making assumptions where no concrete evidence existed and highlighting the gaps to be filled if they were to trace the killer of the British agent John Vince.

They decided to assume that everything Autriche had told Vince at the Pub Bliss was close enough to the truth to be taken as fact, not least because there was no evidence to disprove it. François volunteered to summarise.

"Trump is elected in 2016 and upsets the Democrats. Then he offends the CIA and sacks some of their top men. The extreme right of the Democrats will stop at nothing to get rid of Trump. Security is too tight to consider getting rid of him in the States, but his intended visit to Paris in June 2017 is another matter.

"Somehow big money is made available to fund an assassination, apparently from a source in the south of France. An approach is made to Maxence, a big shot in DGSI, but already known to the CIA and someone with a suspect track record.

"Maxence approaches Autriche, both a friend and an ex-employee, who wants the job but for reasons as yet unknown is not accepted."

"Stop there a moment, François," interrupted Richard, "it is important to remember that a great deal of what you have said is based on supposition and guesswork."

"Yes of course, but it is a very strong theory and fits the facts as we know them. We are now concentrating on less supposition and more facts. For example, we know that Maxence was not accepted for the job and that he poured his heart out to Vince. We know that Autriche was then murdered and, about the same time, so was Vince.

What we don't know is who ordered Autriche's death or who ordered the Vince killing and who did the killings and what were the motives for each? We don't know for certain that there was a CIA link, or who was the CIA contact, and finally who was, or is Mr Big?"

They looked at each other in mutual frustration. "And how," said François "are we supposed to find all the answers in twenty-eight and one half days?"

*   *   *

"Do you remember Jules?" François asked.

"I could hardly forget him! In that spooky converted barn in Biot? The man that smelt of Pernod and stale sweat, who looked like a tramp and surrounded himself with a gang of thugs? Yes, I can just about remember him!"

"He also sends his regards to you Richard! He hopes that you found your friend. Anyway, like you, he is one of my friends; as you know I have eclectic tastes!

I promise you I have not told him anything about our project, but it occurred to me that he would know far more than I about any underground killings that have taken place recently. Jules' little crowd of painters includes some out and out criminals to be sure and I know most of them but they are just on the fringes of the underground world. All I asked him was if he knew anything about a killing a few months ago where the police found a body in the northern suburbs, badly disfigured and tortured.

As Jules said, killings between gang members are not that uncommon but killings involving torture are very rare. It takes a very sick mentality to resort to torture. It is not unknown of course but no-one in Jules circle is that depraved. At the other end of the scale though, there is an extremely unpleasant low life faction, mainly drug related, where nothing is out of bounds. Jules contacted me yesterday. He had put the word out and sure enough there had been strong rumours circulating of just such a killing. The rumours soon died away of course, as they always do. But not before one cretin boasted about being part of the gang involved as if it were something to be proud of!"

"You think it was Autriche?"

"Almost certainly. Three things of particular interest. One: the man killed was hated by a number of people who thought good riddance to bad rubbish, as the English would say, and two: gossip had it that the man was working for the Security Services!"

"You said there were three things?" Richard reminded François.

"Oh, yes! This may interest us Richard. The man thought it was a huge laugh that they were paid in US dollars!"

*   *   *

François said, "I think I am by far the most valuable one of our partnership!"

"Now what?" Richard was showing his irritation at François' superior tone. He was uncomfortably aware that he had contributed absolutely nothing of value to date in their efforts to find a way forward.

"What if I tell you that I have found out how you can meet Maxence?"

"How I can meet him! Do you intend taking a back seat from now on then?"

François totally ignored his friend.

"I know where Maxence spends most of his evenings and I can arrange for you to be there! He is a compulsive gambler and a member of "Jouers du Monde" in Riquier, a suburb in the old town. You have to be a member, but I know the owner so there is no problem. Shall we say tomorrow night?"

"We shall say nothing of the sort, François! How did you find all this out anyway? And why should I be the one to go when you would be the obvious choice?"

"You remember my friend, I do not disclose my sources and I cannot go as there is a serious threat I would be recognised. You on the other hand are a total unknown!"

"You really should apply for a position in the 'Corps Diplomatique'!" Richard observed.

*   *   *

It had been agreed that Richard was a freelance journalist gathering information on the night life of various European cities, of which Nice was one. However improbable the story was, so François said, it had been readily accepted by the manager of the club that Richard should present himself at ten o'clock that Wednesday night.

Richard had ceased to be amazed at the number of friends and acquaintances of François and their obvious readiness to help out when the occasion demanded.

He, Richard, could not start to fathom the nature of their relationships or whether they involved the repayment of past favours granted, or the payment of considerable sums of money and on balance, he did not want to know.

It was a pleasant late September night as he made his way northwards along the Quai Lunel, leaving the Port of Nice on his right as he made his way inland. In his view the area was devoid of character and even at this late hour he was aware of the pollution caused by the day-time traffic, which still hung in the air.

The lights of the moored shipping twinkling in the quays did not, in his view, relieve the general gloom of the area. All around him were static silhouettes of parked massive earth movers and mobile cranes with their silent jibs threateningly poised above the diminished houses and office blocks beneath. All around were unpleasant steel fences grudgingly allowing the occasional exits to those pedestrians who dared to thread their ways through the labyrinths of the construction site which would be filled with noise, dust and oaths when work recommenced in the morning. To Richard it was all too depressing and typified by a crude notice fashioned by some semi-literate workman which, in garish red paint, pointed the way to the now desecrated "Place de Beauté".

The buildings beyond had, in the past displayed a certain splendour; tall imposing office and residential blocks designed by architects and faithfully built to last. Here and there were interspersed signs of current life; the occasional night club; the still occupied flats with the dwellers listed by names and flat numbers, inviting visitors to press for entry. As for the rest, many had been colour-washed with a uniform sand textured finish, but that had been many years ago and neither owners nor occupants had seen fit to refresh the paint, allowing a uniformed grubbiness to hold sway.

The entrance to "Joueurs du Monde" was a pleasant surprise. Discreetly positioned, the plate glass entrance door displayed the name of the club in unobtrusive lettering. To the right was the entry button and he imagined, rather than saw, the CCTV cameras hidden in the ivy across the top of the door.

He and François had discussed both the risks and the futilities of a chance meeting with Maxence. The risks were obvious; he was a dangerous man with a great deal to lose. The futilities were if either the meeting did not even occur or any such meeting proved valueless.

They agreed that Richard could at least assess the man, both his character and his weaknesses, which would hopefully show them a way to move forward.

They both agreed that the risks far outweighed the possible rewards but then the available time was desperately short.

Richard hesitated for a few seconds and then pressed the bell.

*　　*　　*

The furnishings would have done credit to a five-star hotel. Subdued lighting cast a warm glow on the soft leather armchairs and the occasional tables were adorned with the current issues of high-life magazines.

One corner of the room was occupied by a purpose built bar and four bar stools, while at the far end of the room open double doors framed a view of the gaming tables beyond. To the left of the doors was an unobtrusive desk and chair behind which a substantial safe had been encased into the deep wall.

Pierre was a swarthy thick set man of indeterminate age, a weather tanned face and surprisingly blue eyes of a startling intensity and a welcoming smile with which he greeted Richard.

"We do not open before half-past ten," he explained, "my staff will be here in the next quarter of an hour or so and I thought it best for us to meet a little earlier."

He was immaculately dressed in an expensive two piece suit and a dove grey tie. Richard immediately apologised for his comparatively shoddy wear with his faded, albeit respectable, jacket.

Pierre laughed.

"My dear Richard – may I call you that? The days of gambling casinos with dinner jackets and bow ties are long gone. To stay in business these days we have to accept all sorts of dress and indeed the fact that you are wearing a collar and tie puts you in the higher echelon of my clientele!"

"It is good of you to accommodate me Pierre. If I may say so your English is impeccable! I thought I may have to struggle with my imperfect French!"

"The education provided by some of your public schools is beyond reproach," said Pierre, "I have a lot to thank Winchester College for!"

Richard looked sharply at the other man but could detect no irony or sarcasm. In any case he had never had cause to disclose his background to François. It was, nevertheless, an uncomfortable coincidence.

"Now, Richard," Pierre went on, "I gather that you are collecting material for this book of yours and you are travelling Europe to gain an insight into the differing nightlife on offer?"

"Something like that. I have now retired so I have time to spare and I have always wanted to travel in Europe."

Pierre seemed to accept him at face value, accepting who he was and the reasons for his visit without demur. Richard could not identify whether Pierre was just being himself or play-acting his part in the story spun by François. Either way he felt secure enough to relax in Pierre's company as he explained the so called house rules; no smoking anywhere; members and partners only, dress code smart casual, no ladies allowed at gaming tables, drinks on credit at tables to be settled before departure, no fraternisation with staff, maximum losses at tables as agreed with member on registration; all losses to be settled monthly unless otherwise agreed by management.

"You, of course, are a special guest of mine but you can appreciate that you will not be allowed into the gaming rooms. I hope, none-theless, you will have a worthwhile evening."

"I am interested to find out the nature of the people who come here and their attitudes to gambling. Don't get me wrong, Pierre. I do not intend asking anyone any questions! I just want to observe. I am already picking up differences in characters, not only from country to country but even from city to city. If you sense any awkwardness though, do feel free to throw me out!"

"Don't worry, I will! I have some able assistance on hand, as you can see." He waved his hand in the general direction of two well built young man already looking uncomfortable in their close fitting jackets. As he was to be confined to the ante-room he decided to look the part and, much to the relief of Pierre, paying for a bottle of Macallan malt whisky. He could think of worse ways to spend an evening as he downed his first scotch and appreciated Pierre's good taste in employing such attractive waitresses.

Early newcomers drifted in soon after eleven o'clock, mainly men without partners but all being members who knew each other, either by sight or name. They barely acknowledged Richard's existence, who was comfortably seated alongside a coffee table in one corner of the room. To his relief no background music interfered with the conversational buzz and the ambience was one of comfortable sophistication.

Pierre had just stopped by Richard's table to exchange pleasantries when Maxence arrived, or more accurately, burst upon the scene. There was no mistaking his identity as a number of members called out to him as he crossed the room. He was a big man with a big presence and, as it too soon became clear, a big ego.

Richard had no pre-conceived ideas of the man who must have been in his mid-sixties with a florid complexion and a loud but well educated voice. Seeing Pierre he came across to address the manager, completely ignoring Richard's existence.

"Pierre, il n'y a personne qui aide aux tables de jeu. Pourqois pas?"

"Je suis desolé. Monsieur. Je vais y assiste. En attendant, puis je vous présenter Richard, mon ami anglais?"

"My pleasure" said Maxence in impeccable English. "Do you play the tables, Monsieur?"

"Regrettably no," Richard replied, "I am just here in Nice on a short holiday and Pierre kindly asked if I would like to join him one evening. I am hoping to write a book about the night-life in European cities."

"Bonne chance, Monsieur." Maxence turned to the manager but continued in English. "Pierre, as you will see I have brought a companion with me tonight!"

He waved across the room to an attractive and well dressed woman in her mid thirties to join him.

"Jeanette, may I introduce you to Monsieur le Directeur, Pierre, and also to his English friend, Richard?"

"Enchanté" said Richard and Pierre, almost as one.

"Now, Pierre," Maxence said brusquely, "I take it that Jeanette can accompany me to the tables?"

"Malheuresement non, Monsieur." Then, remembering Richard's presence "I am afraid it is the rule of the house, as you know Monsieur. No ladies in the gaming room."

"You forget who I am Monsieur. I wish Jeanette to accompany me, is that understood?"

"I am sorry, Monsieur, it is not possible!"

Richard could see that Maxence was about to explode in temper when the lady in question intervened.

"Non, Maxence, ce n'est pas important. Je preférè tu pour gagner beaucoup d,argent pour nous de dépensèr! En tout cas je ne comprehends pas du jeu. Je trouve qu'il soit plus agréable de prendre un verre avec Pierre and Richard! Vraiment!"

Richard could see Maxence struggling with his emotions. He was obviously keen to challenge Pierre further but his addiction to gambling won him over. Grudgingly he agreed and he disappeared with Pierre to try his skills.

Jeanette smiled warmly at Richard. "So you have me for the evening!"and he smiled at her English which to him had so many meanings.

Most of the men had now drifted into the gambling hall, either to try the tables or to watch, including Pierre and his bouncers. Two middle aged business men remained seated on bar stools, arguing over some complex trade deal and evidently not being interested in gambling that evening.

Jeanette was the only woman present and by club rules had to stay in the ante-room, along with Richard. As a courtesy he offered her a drink which she readily accepted, having no wish to sit in isolation.

They exchanged pleasantries and discussed various inconsequential mundane matters. Each relaxed as they chatted, assisted by his whisky and her pina coladas.

"So what is your link with Monsieur Moreau?" Richard asked.

"I have known Maxence for a number of years "Jeanette explained, "It is what you call an on/off relationship. Off for most of the time but on when he feels lonely, depressed, bored or generally in need of company or sex."

She saw Richard's startled reaction and laughed.

"Let's not fool ourselves, Richard. I am in fact a call girl but I would like to think a high class one. At least I charge Maxence a great deal of money!"

It was Richards turn to laugh, albeit a little nervously.

"You have thrown me a bit," he admitted. "I would not have guessed, particularly with your fluent English."

"In my profession you need to be at least bi-lingual. Anyway I am becoming tired of Max, I could do with a change. Perhaps with an Englishman?" she asked coquettishly. "Max is loud, bad mannered, drinks too much and thinks too much about himself but he is very, very rich!"

Richard enjoyed the mild flirtation.

"I am not sure I am any of those things," he said, "and I am certainly not rich!"

"The nice ones never are," she said, "but being rich is very, very important!"

"You could always marry him!" Richard suggested.

"Even I have my limits," she replied, "and that would be a step too far even for me! Besides he has a regular mistress, or so he says, but from what he tells me they are always rowing and he probably only sees her about once a month. Mind you, the latest row does seem to be quite serious. I don't think he has seen her for two or three months and he is always in a foul temper these days, so who knows?"

"Tell me, as we obviously have plenty of time to spare," he looked at his watch; already well over an hour had passed, "what does he do for a living? Come to that what does his so-called mistress do? Have you ever met her?"

"Good heavens no, and I have no wish to. That would break all the rules wouldn't it?

I have no idea what he does and I have given up being interested. Her name is Arianne; I can always remember that! Did you know that it is taken from the Latin 'Ariadne' which means 'utterly pure'. I mean, come off it, she is as pure as I am!"

Richard smiled; the claws were certainly out now.

"Max did say something when we first met about her being a French-Canadian, I think it was. She works in Nice, I know that, and is about ten years younger than him. And he said something about it being very difficult for them to meet due to his job, whatever that meant!"

As she finished speaking the gaming room doors were flung open and a very worried looking Pierre came out, followed by his two henchman who were both trying to support and propel a very drunk and voluble Maxence.

"Now sit down, Monsieur, if you please!" commanded a very agitated Pierrre, "and please moderate your language, there is a lady present!"

"Do you mean Jeanette? Pah!" Maxence shouted, but minutes later fell almost silent, mumbling incomprehensively to himself while the two men manoeuvred him into a vacant armchair. Jeanette hesitated but then decided her place was next to Maxence whom she approached with a look of disgust on her face.

"Is there anything I can do to help?" asked Richard.

"There is nothing anyone can do until he sobers up!" Pierre replied, "This is as bad as I have seen him recently. Over the last few months he has been impossible. This time he drank too much, gambled too much and lost almost everything. I should have banned him from the club before now!"

By now Jeannette had joined them, having given up her attempts to calm Maxence.

"Can we get him a taxi? If I can get him home, at least I can put him to bed!"

"Not on your own, you won't Madame. I will tell one of my men to go with you. Whatever it was that customer said to him tipped him right over the edge. I must be certain he is not a danger to himself or to anyone else before I let him go. Otherwise I must call the police and arrange for an ambulance."

One of the customers who had been in the gaming room detached himself from the small group in the corner of the bar and came across to Pierre, accosting him in French.

"What was that all about?" Richard asked Jeanette.

"He said he was the man who tried to reason with Max. He

obviously knows him well and in trying to calm him down spoke about Max's family. Apparently Max flew into an unbelievable rage and the man thought Max was going to have a heart attack! Apparently all the man said was whether Max had seen Marcel recently and how was he?"

"And who, then, is Marcel?"

Jeanette stared at Richard deciding how much she should say to a total stranger. The she shrugged her shoulders, as if to say it was of little consequence now.

"Most people don't know this but Max has an adopted son. He goes under the name of Marcel Autriche."

CHAPTER TWENTY-SEVEN

"Sian, I have been trying to get hold of Tom without success, any idea where he might be?"

"Sorry, Dad. I meant to tell you. He has had to go to London to see his father who is not at all well."

"I am sorry to hear it," said Peter, "but I have never heard him talk about his parents before. To be honest I had no idea Tom had any living relatives!"

"No, he certainly doesn't talk about them very much. He once told me his mother died a few years ago, but I have never heard anything about his father before."

"At long last I got round to calling in on Winchester Hospital to pick up the letter from Amy. I am sure we all want to know what is in it!"

"What… haven't you read it? I would be busting to open it and see how the story ends!"

"No. I thought it was something we should all share. So I was going to call a meeting and open it then. Problem is Richard isn't here either and he really was the founding father of our secret exploration. Do you know when Tom might be back?"

"I don't think he knows himself but I think perhaps a few days."

"Well, the last I heard from Richard he was very definite that he would be home by the end of the month. That is only two and half weeks away from now. I am inclined to leave the opening of Amy's letter until we are all present; it seems only fair!"

Reluctantly Sian agreed. She was dying to read the letter but the Curious Case of the Headstone deserved a suitable closure in front of them all.

*   *   *

Tom had struggled to pay for the seven-year old Citreon when he bought it three years ago and thought the sat-nav was an unnecessary luxury. Not so now; there was no other way he could have found his way through the streets of London and beyond in his search for the hospital.

The 'phone call came totally out of the blue. He had not seen or spoken to his father for over twenty years, indeed he had no idea whether he was alive or dead and in truth was not particularly interested. It was the hospital secretary who had rung him explaining his father was receiving palliative care and unlikely to live for more than a few weeks. They had had major problems in tracking him down and Tom was still unclear how they managed it.

With very mixed emotions he had reluctantly agreed to the visit, not even sure he would recognise his father or what there was for them to talk about.

He was relieved to learn that 'Mr Charles Wakefield' had his own private room; Tom had been dreading a meeting in a general ward.

A young, competent nurse showed him the way, instructing him not to overstay his visit "as Mr Southern tires very easily these days."

Of course he recognised his own father. He had only been ten years old at the time but he remembered his eyes and the slight smile that forever seemed to play on his lips. There had been a number of photographs kept by his mother until she had died at the obscenely early age of forty-eight.

They looked at each other in momentary silence and then came the smile.

"Hello Tom, I am glad you came!"

Tom could not return the smile. The memories came flooding back and he heard himself struggling to suppress his emotions.

"The hospital said you were not very well; it has been a long time!"

"Yes, far too long. Your mother stayed in touch with me for a while but she said you never wanted to see of hear from me again and I promised to stay out of your life."

"It was your decision Dad, and not for me to interfere. Let's just say I had difficulty in dealing with it all and what it did to Mum. Better that we stayed apart and lived our own lives."

"If you say so, Tom. It's all water under the bridge now, of course, but I broke my promise to your mother by asking the hospital to contact you. I know that, but being told you only have a few weeks to live does change your perspective."

"Yes, I am sure it does and I think I am glad you did. It would have been uncomfortable not to meet up and clear the air before it was too late. I can see that now."

"Thank you Tom, I appreciate it. As this will be the last occasion for us to talk, would you tell me why you think I left home and your mother?"

"Dad, it's all years ago now and I'm not sure I see the point. Mum told me you had had, or were having, an affair and all in all you decided you should go and leave her to bring me up."

His father fell silent taking in what his son had just told him.

"Maybe we should just leave it at that Tom, but did it occur to you there might be another side to the story?"

"No, not really, are you saying there was?"

"Put it this way Tom. Suppose I said that it was your mother that had an affair and I just could not live with it. Suppose she and I agreed that I would take all the blame so that your life would not be too damaged by the fallout. Would you have believed that?"

Tom stared at his father.

"Why should I, Dad? Don't you think I have been through enough? Mum is dead so only you know the truth. I think perhaps this meeting does not seem such a good idea after all. Let's leave it at that shall we?"

He took one last look at his father and left the room.

He cried most of the way home to Hampshire.

CHAPTER TWENTY-EIGHT

"Take me through that again!" François demanded. "A little more slowly this time, if you don't mind. I am not sure I really understand any part of it!"

"I know," said Richard, "I thought for a moment I had misheard, but on thinking it through it does explain a number of things that weren't making sense. This call girl, which is what she calls herself, has known Maxence for a number of years and obviously knows him extremely well. She doesn't particularly like him but she does like his money and what it brings. She has a strange sort of honesty about her; she understands the reality of everyday life and has few illusions about it. She accepts people for what they are and I both like her and believe her."

"Obviously," said François.

"Think about it, François. Maxence by all accounts seemed to think that the sun shone out of Marcel Autriche's backside. The relationship was not just employer and employee. Think how he fought to keep Autriche from getting fired when the DGSI went through its reorganisation in 2014. On the face of it there was more than enough evidence to fire him on the spot but Maxence must have put his own career in jeopardy by defending him the way he did. Even after Autriche was dismissed Maxence kept close contact with him, the rumour being that Autriche had too many useful under-ground contacts to lose. But what if they were father and son?

"What I saw last night was a man emotionally destroyed. Agreed he had had far too much to drink; indeed he was half cut when he first came into the club, but that was different. This was not anger or triumphalism. This was genuine grief and I don't believe for one moment that he tortured and murdered his own son."

"What was the name of the long term mistress? Not the call-girl, the other one."

"Arianne. Why?"

"It seems to me that if we are going to take Maxence off the list then we should talk to her. I will see what I can find out."

Pierre confirmed to François that he was legally bound to have a register of members and their addresses which he would show only to the police when requested but to no-one else. He watched while François copied out the details which François then showed to Richard.

"This is Maxence's address in Vence. Pierre said that he also has a company flat in Nice which he uses for most of the time. So my guess is that Arianne lives at his place in Vence."

"Perhaps, but listen to this! You may not remember but when Maxence was investigated in 2012 by his bosses the accusation was that he had too close an association with someone in a firm called 'Marchandises. S.A'. MI6 discovered that this was a front company for the CIA, hence all the hoo-hah. MI6 did look into this more closely but could not be bothered to tell us at the time, of course! My contact there tells me that the listed company 'Directrice' is none other than Arianne Fournier."

François let out a whistle.

"Well, it is all starting to add up," he said, "but surely she would not now be living with him, in view of the enquiry which closed; if I recall correctly for 'lack of evidence'. What more evidence do you need?"

"Don't forget," Richard replied, "that the enquiry was over five years ago. I am sure they were not living together at the time but after a number of years? People move on, memories fade and what was considered unacceptable then would not raise a second glance now!"

"True," François agreed. "Somehow we need to see her, but how exactly? What about you barging in on her and saying 'I represent the British security service and I think you know who killed my friend, so tell me all!' ".

"Do you think that would be too subtle?" Richard asked.

*   *   *

"Thinking about it," Richard said, "I don't see how we can knock on Arianne's door in Vence and ask for a chat! On what grounds? Who do we say we represent?"

"I know, hence my silly example of you barging in and showing your MI5 badge! But she is the key to all this, I am sure of that. I do have some ideas but none of them can involve you my friend! I think there is a faint chance that I could get in to see her on my own but there is no way I can explain your presence as well. No disrespect Richard, but your French is hardly out of the Sorbonne and will not be able to cope with the argot commonly used around these parts!"

"Don't worry François, I am only slightly offended! Knowing you, I can well believe that with your Gaelic charm and devastatng good looks that you can bluff your way into most places, but I am not letting you go to Vence on your own!"

"Let me work on it, Richard, I have a few 'phone calls to make, but let's hope we can set off for Vence; say in one hour's time?"

*   *   *

"Right," said François, "all organised. Our friend Pierre has confirmed that Maxence is at his office in Nice and that Arianne is in Vence at Maxence's flat. So far so good, and I have hired a car; I will drive. Allons-y!"

"And how did Pierre manage that?" Richard asked.

"Easy; he spoke to Arianne and explained that he had something of Max's which he had left at the club and that a friend of his, moi-meme, naturellement, would be dropping it off, as I would be in Vence today. Maxence is not expected home tonight, it would seem. C'est un coup de chance, n'est-ce-pas. Richard?"

*   *   *

"Did you remember to bring whatever it was that Maxence left at the club?" Richard asked as they waited in a traffic jam on the outskirts of Nice.

"But of course, it is there on the back seat."

The Frenchman pointed to the small good quality case which looked like hundreds of others seen in the City areas.

"Open it if you wish!"

Richard caught his breath at the sight of the 50 Euro notes bound in rubber bands.

"What the…?"

"Good thinking eh, my friend? What perhaps one could expect to take away from a gambling club? If one won of course. Very useful if I have to bribe to get the information we need!"

"Dare I ask where you got these from?"

"Oh, from someone who does not need them anymore. They may come in quite useful!"

The traffic cleared and within the hour they were on the outskirts of Vence. François drove confidently and explained he knew exactly the location of the flat they were seeking.

"It is in an area I know reasonably well," he explained. "It is just round the corner from a favourite restaurant of mine, L'Ambroisie on the Avenue Alphonse Toreille. We will park the car outside the restaurant and you will take a table to wait for me there while I will see if Arianne will see me. I should be back within the hour. If for any reason I am not then you can come to find me, if you have to. I have written the address on the envelope I will give you when we park. Seriously though my friend, be very careful, we have no idea what we are going to find!"

*   *   *

Richard finished his drink and looked at his watch. It was well past the hour that François had stipulated and with some trepidation he found the envelope containing the address and made his way to the restaurant door. He apologised profusely to the waiter, explaining that his friend had obviously got the wrong date, paid for the bottle of Perrier water and added ten euros as a tip.

He found the address easily enough. As François had said it was only a stone's throw from the restaurant and he stood assessing the Georgian three storey house standing in its own grounds.

"Some flat," he thought to himself, "very nice!"

After he had rung the bell he waited a few minutes before a male voice boomed through the intercom.

"Qui est la? Que veux tu?"

Richard paused. He had not expected a male voice. Surely Maxence had not returned? Now what?

"Mon nom est Merrington," he stumbled and then realised that his French was totally inadequate for the situation. He continued in English.

"I was given this address by my friend, who I think may still be with you?"

Then in a defiant attempt to pretend he was bilingual "Je peux entrer?"

He could hear indistinct voices in the background and then a silence which seemed to go on for ever.

Then a female voice, this time in English. "Wait for a few moments, I will come down."

It was at least five minutes before there was any sense of movement, The noise of bolts being pulled back and the door being opened by no more than a few centi-metres, held fast by the security chain.

The same female voice asked, nervously, "Are you on your own?"

"Yes, you can see that. Will you open the door for me?"

Another wait. The security chain was released. As the door opened Richard was blinded by the torchlight shone straight onto his eyes. A hand grabbed the lapels of his jacket and pulled him violently inside and the door was slammed shut behind him. The torch was switched off and he was immersed in impenetrable darkness.

A man's voice barked some instructions in argot.

The woman said, "Face the wall and put your hands up, palms on the wall!"

Male hands frisked him roughly and invasively.

"Hands behind your back... slowly!" said the woman.

His hands were seized and coarse twining rope burnt into his skin as his wrists were lashed together.

"Go up the stairs and if you make any attempt to escape, you will be hurt, badly!"

He stumbled up the unfamiliar stairs and was shoved violently into the room facing the stairwell.

"Nice of you to drop in, old boy," said François, "Better late than never!"

*　　*　　*

"The good news," said François, gesturing at the masked men sitting at the end of the room, "is that neither of these two apes speaks a word of English! And that is the end of the good news, I'm afraid. So while you and I chat bear in mind that the gorgeous Arianne is over there," and he smiled warmly at the woman, "and is fluent if not in English, certainly in American and apparently can hear a pin drop from twenty metres away."

By no stretch of the imagination could Richard have called Arianne gorgeous. In her fifties it was possible that seven years ago she would have had an appeal but by no means could she claim, like Cleopatra, 'that age had not withered her.'

She was sitting on the floor in one corner of the room with Richard and François opposite her and the masked men guarding the door at the far end.

She did not seem to be talking to them and her eyes were puffed up, apparently with crying; spasmodically her shoulders would heave as she suppressed her sobs.

"Were the two thugs here when you arrived François?"

"No, I had been with Arienne for over half an hour when they arrived. She must have recognised one of them, pressed the door release and both of them pushed through, roughed her up a bit and told her to sit where she is now. They said very little but I am guessing they were hoping to find Maxence here. She told them she had no idea where he was or when he is likely to be back and that is probably true. I have the feeling they are not sure what to do next, sit and hope he turns up or 'phone for further instructions."

Richard looked carefully at the two men. Both wore balaclavas which successfully masked any distinguishing features. The slimmer of the two had dark brown eyes and Richard glimpsed a swarthy skin which indicated an Asian or African connection, while the other man was both large and tall, white with an unshaven face.

They were both sitting on chairs pulled from the dining room table which ran lengthways down the room. Apart from a large sideboard on the far wall the room was curiously devoid of furniture. Both men were scruffily dressed, one in jeans and a mis-shapen jumper, the other with a dark mud-splattered overall and a roll neck beneath. Both men wore trainers.

On his lap the larger of the two men held a semi-automatic rifle pointing in the general direction of Richard and François There was also a handgun held loosely in the left hand of the other man. Their silence was unnerving.

"Is the woman on their side or ours?" whispered Richard.

"Probably not on ours. She believes we are 'videurs', or bouncers, from Les Jouers, or the police in some form or other. Either way I am not sure we would have much support if we needed it. She is certainly not on their side, though, they have already roughed her up once!"

"I don't think those cretins consider us much of a threat," observed Richard, "they haven't even bothered to tie our legs together!"

"What do you suggest we do then? Ram them with our heads while they are reloading?" François mocked.

"If Arianne is not on our side I guess she won't do anything to help them either!" said Richard.

"Maybe not," Francois agreed, "but I have no wish to be a dead hero even if you have! Let's see what happens; they might even let us go!"

"Do you believe that?" asked Richard.

"Not for a single second but I am always an optimist!"

The shrill ring tone of the man's mobile startled everyone in the room.

"Oui; ç'est moi. Avez vous décidé à quoi faire de deux hommes dont je vous ai parlé plus tôt? O.K. – et la femme? Je comprends."

François turned to Richard and whispered "He asked what he should do with us, that is all I heard. I am guessing it won't be good news."

"We can't just sit here like a couple of dummies waiting to find out!" Richard whispered back, "I don't mind a heat butt, if it helps!"

François smiled back.

"Let's make it up as we go along. Happy for me to pick the moment?"

"Bien sûr François. Just give me the word!"

The two gangsters had by now resumed their seats, still training their armoury towards Richard and Francois.

Some ten minutes later the younger of the two stood up and placed the handgun on the chair.

"Il me faut a pisser!" he exclaimed to his companion, who nodded his agreement, and the younger man left the room.

"Now, Richard, now!" yelled François.

They struggled to get to their feet as best as they could with their arms tied behind their backs and hurled themselves at the remaining man. Francois being younger and fitter raced ahead of Richard at the startled man who, while standing up, fumbled with the semi-automatic. François was now almost on top of him when he fired. He could not miss and the impetus of the wounded François bought them both crashing to the floor, the rifle torn from the gunman's grasp. He managed to roll free of François' fallen body and desperately scrambled for the fallen rifle a few yards away.

Richard, hands still tied behind his back. could do nothing for his friend, so he threw himself bodily onto the gunman and heard the gratifying sound of broken ribs which were not his. The man gurgled and lost consciousness.

To his left Richard could see the handgun on the vacant chair and knew, with his hands still tied behind his back, that he could do nothing about it.

The door opened as the younger man returned and bent down to reach for his handgun, while Richard looked on helplessly. He sensed, rather than saw, someone to his left as Arianne won the chase, seized the gun and fired it all in one moment.

The gangster screamed as the bullet severed an artery in his neck and within moments he was dying on the floor in a pool of his own blood.

"I will call 112 for an ambulance!" Arianne said in the deafening silence that followed.

*   *   *

Francois was not dead. Half his shoulder had been blown away by the bullet discharged from the rifle but he was not dead. He managed to smile at Richard.

"I told you to look after yourself cretin! You never listen!"

He was semi-consciousness when they moved him into the ambulance.

CHAPTER TWENTY-NINE

Richard gazed out of the window at the Thames moving inexorably towards the sea. He knew he was physically exhausted but in the forty-eight hours since the killing he had not slept. The adrenalin coursed through his veins and ensured that he re-lived every moment as if it was now and not then.

"Are you all right, Richard? Do you want to carry on?"

He turned away from the window and looked at Geoffrey. Pompous Geoffrey trying to struggle through to his pension. He didn't need this, and Richard knew it.

"Fine, thank you, sir. Just a bit tired."

"Of course, but we have to answer some fairly pointed questions upstairs, as you will understand."

"Yes."

He looked at the three of them; Geoffrey, Neil and Bill Smithson. Just people doing their job. Honourable citizens trying to steer through the lies and deceits of a murky world that was rarely honourable.

"As you will know Richard, we have contacted the Nice hospital and François Duval is stable and out of danger. A full review will be carried out on his shoulder to establish the extent of the damage and the surgical options but they are hopeful that a one hundred per cent recovery will be possible."

"I owe him my life," Richard said, "I can't thank him enough!"

"Quite so" said Geoffrey, "in due course we will be examining both your involvement and the unauthorised engagement of Mr Duval in all of this. That however is for another time. I shall now ask Neil to take over to fill in the gaps, as it were, for our internal report. Neil?"

Neil smiled at Richard who sensed a little more warmth in the atmosphere.

"I think these gaps relate almost entirely to the events of that last day. To a point you have been keeping us informed of progress, although there does seem to be a lack of information in the last two weeks!"

"We were a bit busy at the time" Richard offered.

"No doubt. We already have the overall picture of what happened but your objective should have been to establish who was behind the killing of agent John Vince and why. The principal players seem to have been Maxence Moreau, Marcel Autriche and the woman Arianne Caron."

"I never knew her surname!" exclaimed Richard.

"You are forgetting that we have a transcript of the 2012 enquiry regarding Moreau and the girl at Marchandises S.A. Let's start with Maxence Moreau, though, and then Marcel Autriche."

"They were father and illegitimate son but it was a well kept secret. I don't think even the DGSI knew of the link."

"It seems to me," said Neil, "that Maxence was at all times a slightly dodgy character."

"Quite agree. Initially all our focus was on him, and from what we could see he was a man of very few principles. He was the man first contacted about the proposed assassination and easily attracted by the money. He cocked it up, of course, blabbing to his son who blabbed to Vince. That's why they were both killed. But he was hardly going to order his own son's death let alone his torture. That had to be someone else!"

"Which leads us to Arianne. She surely must have been involved?"

Richard shook his head. "I was able to talk to François before the nurse threw me out; he had half an hour with Arianne before the gangsters broke in. François is convinced that she was no more than a pawn in the whole business. She worked at Marchandises, yes, but only as a PA to her Nice boss, whoever he was at the time. He knew that she was having an affair with Maxence and he also knew that Maxence could be bribed. What better way to muddy the waters than to channel the idea of the assassination through someone linked with the DGSI and who had detailed knowledge of the French underworld? That way, politically, the assassination would be linked to the French, not the United States."

"Are you saying she knew nothing about it?"

"Nothing of any relevance. She was told by her boss to see whether Maxence would be interested in a project which involved, potentially, millions of dollars. If so, he was instructed to make direct contact with whoever was putting up the money. We have not been able to identify who this was and of course it may just have been an agent or indeed Mr Big himself!"

"Mr Big?" interrupted Geoffrey. "What sort of name is that? It's like something straight out of a children's comic!"

"Actually" Bill Smithson interjected. "It was the name of a pop metal band formed in the late 1980s."

Everyone looked at Smithson in amazement.

"Well that proves it," Geoffrey spluttered, "we are not having that name in any of our reports. Whatever next!"

"It was very successful in Japan," persisted Bill, as if that had any relevance whatsoever to the purpose of the meeting.

"Moving on," said Neil, "are you saying, Richard, that the woman can be discounted?"

François thinks so; the only point she played was to pass on the message to Maxence. We think he probably told her in pillow talk about the scheme, at least in outline, because he is that sort of person, but she claims to know nothing about the source of the fund or the identity of, do excuse me, sir, Mr Big. She is a weak sort of person, probably a reasonable PA but that is about it, in our view. We do know that Maxence told her about Autriche's death because that is when Maxence fell apart and disappeared from her life. I tried to identify the name of her boss who was clearly much involved, but for reasons as yet unknown she refused to give it. She did say that he was recalled to Washington in June or July this year which coincides with the failure of the assassination attempt. He has since been replaced by some faceless nominee of the CIA, or so I gather. I did not push her too hard as I realised that the political implications of American money was beyond my pay grade!"

"And beyond ours too, I reckon," said Neil, "that is DG material and best left alone. Do we know for sure that it was American money?"

"We have no proof of that, obviously," Richard replied, "but if we link the Trump visit to Paris with a CIA front office in Marchandises S.A and the promise of almost unlimited funds for a successful assassination, we think it is almost a slam dunk!"

"Slam what?" Geoffrey could not keep quiet. "There you go again Richard! There is no excuse for using a language that has only existed for three hundred years or so! Good God, slam dunk, indeed!"

"We can tidy this up later," Neil reasoned, "but we get the general idea, Richard. So getting back to the purpose of all this, who killed John Vince and why?"

"We still don't know," Richard admitted, "but I think we can safely say why. Autriche thought he had the contract for assassination and suddenly it is taken out of his grasp. He does not pass muster for whatever reason, and yet Mr Big – I am sorry, sir, I cannot think of an alternative – realises that not only Maxence knows of the plan but so does Autriche, who may have told others. So Autriche is tortured to find out who he talked to, then killed him, and then traced John Vince and killed him too."

"But why is Maxence left alone by the death squad?" Bill had decided he ought to make a contribution, "He was to blame for the whole shambles!"

"Because they had him hog-tied. At any moment they could destroy him professionally and bring his world crashing down around his ears and if necessary remove him in the same way they tortured and killed Autriche and executed John Vince. It was those deaths that guaranteed Maxence would never again talk to another outsider!"

"But he is still there," Bill pointed out, "and as a senior member of the DGSI he could still cause immense damage!"

Geoffrey quickly butted in.

"We don't need to bother about that now, it is all under control."

Richard stared at Geoffrey, failing to understand what he implied but before he could ask his question Neil continued.

"So Richard, are we to understand that despite your efforts we still have no clear answers as to who or why?"

"That is not entirely fair. We know why our agent was killed – because that miserable Autriche insisted on drunkenly broadcasting his own misfortunes in such a public place. And we effectively know who killed him; some low-life member of the gang who had previously tortured Autriche."

"We still don't know the identity of this Mr Big who ordered the killing," Neil pointed out.

"Who also promised to underwrite the cost of an assassination attempt. No we don't, although my guess is that it was an extremely wealthy donor of the American Democratic Party."

"But you can't prove it and you can't name him!" Neil persisted.

"Well mark it down as a failure, then. I really don't give a shit!"

Geoffrey actually smiled

"At least you are using Anglo-Saxon language now, Richard. I actually think you and Mr Duval did extremely well. It is a blessing in disguise that we can't put a finger on this man's identity. At least now we have nothing to tell the Yanks; so no political repercussions."

"There is just one thing though," Richard said slowly. "When Arianne was eliminating the young gangster, I took the opportunity of the kicking the mobile phone along the floor for her to pick up. This is the one that was used by the other man to ring for his further instructions. As far as I know it was the only call he made. Maybe your boffins can trace it and for all I know could identify the caller. It could even be Mr Big himself!" He smiled sweetly at Geoffrey, produced the phone from his pocket and laid it on the table in front of them.

Geoffrey looked at Neil and Neil looked at Geoffrey.

"Congratulations Richard, but I don't think our boys will get anything from it, do you Neil?"

"'fraid not boss – but as you say, well done Richard!" said Neil.

It took Richard a few moments to grasp the underlying message. No; there would be no international reper-cussions after all.

"What about Maxence?" he asked, "You said we need not bother ourselves about him?"

"Ah, yes Richard. I cannot tell you too much but I am authorised to tell you one thing. Your friend Francois Duval is a very high ranking member of the DGSI and he was already on Maxence's trail when you met him."

CHAPTER THIRTY

"I thought you said that Richard would be here by now!" Sian petulantly challenged her father.

Peter smiled knowingly at her.

"He is actually on his way as we speak. I spoke to him very briefly this morning and he reckons to be home by this evening. He also said all he wanted to do was sleep for twenty four hours so I am afraid, my girl, that you will have to curb your soul in patience until after the weekend!"

Sian found herself blushing, as if she had been caught out in some girlish prank.

"I was only asking Dad, that's all! You would have thought after so long in the south of France his batteries would be fully charged!"

"I don't think it was that sort of holiday," Peter replied, "and while we are on the subject Sian, I would be grateful if you and Tom could avoid quizzing him too much about his time abroad. All I am prepared to say is that he has not exactly had a fun time."

Sian looked pensively at her father.

"You know more than you are letting on, aren't you?"

"Perhaps. Though provided you and Tom agree with my request then no more need be said on the subject."

"If you say so, of course, and I guarantee that Tom will also agree. Anyway as you know Dad, social chit chat is hardly his scene!"

"For the record Sian, how are you and Tom getting on now?"

"We are very good friends and that is how it will be going forward. We have had a long chat about things and it was a pleasant surprise that Tom fully agreed and had been holding back on the subject. All is fine between us and anyway he is carving out a career for himself! He has signed up to do a degree in husbandry, so we won't see that much of him in the future. His father died recently and left him a considerable amount of money, so he tells me. Tom was embarrassed by it all because the last time he saw his father they parted on very bad terms. It had not occurred to Tom that there was any money or that it would come to him. So he is determined to put it to good use."

"I am pleased for him," said Peter, "apart from that time when we had the meeting at your flat, did you invite him over again?"

"You know far better than to ask, Dad, and I have no intention of answering!"

*   *   *

Richard opened his eyes, rolled out of bed groggily, stood up and yawned. Daylight was showing in the chinks of the curtains which he pulled open whilst checking his watch.

Despite his threat to Peter to sleep for twenty-four hours he had only managed ten, but to him it seemed like the sleep of the dead. His eyes had closed the minute his head had touched the pillow and he had had a dreamless sleep until some slight noise had woken him at the respectable hour of nine o'clock on a Sunday morning.

His first thought was that his dog had disturbed him but then he remembered that Buster was still being cared for by Peter and had been so for some weeks.

The small lawn outside his house was covered in frost but the winter sun showed promised that it would be a fine day for early November. To Richard it seemed light years away from the remaining warmth of the Riveria which he had only left two days before.

He knew it would be dark by six o'clock that evening and nearly freezing by early morning but above all else it was home and the place for which he had been yearning throughout these recent days of frenetic and disturbing stress.

He managed to get through to the Nice hospital even on a Sunday morning and had a fifteen minute chat with François, Richard was left with the impression that François had fallen in love with at least three nurses, and they with him. His physical progress had apparently been remarkable and although he would have to return for constructive surgery he was hoping to be no more than an out-patient in a matter of days.

Richard's 'phone call to Peter established that Buster was in rude health and had not missed him in the slightest. Peter invited Richard along with Sian and Tom to an early supper the following evening "with a view to putting a satisfactory end to the case of the Mysterious Headstone enquiry." Peter refused to elucidate.

There really is no place like home Richard decided.

*   *   *

They all thought, although did not say, that Richard looked tired and older than his years and they deter-mined that the first part of the evening would be frothy and light hearted. In this they were aided by Buster who bounced at Richard the moment he walked into the room.

Apart from a "good to see you back" and comparisons between the weather in Nice and the cold snap in the Hampshire village both Sian and Tom kept their promises to Peter.

At his request all discussion on the mysterious headstone was deferred until after supper which Sian had expertly cooked while Peter freely distributed some high class Italian wine.

Tom was full of excitement about his forthcoming studies and Richard could sense the relaxed atmosphere between Tom and Sian which boded well for their newly formed friendship.

They all decided to forego coffee, each in his or her way anticipating the revelation of Amy's letter.

Prior to the supper Peter had bought Richard fully up to date on every development leading up to the evening and Richard was more than pleased to have his mind taken off the south of France, torture and intrigue.

They all helped clear the table and load the dishwasher and resumed their seats to hear Peter start proceedings.

"I want to assure you all," he said rather pompously, "that while I have Amy's last letter in front of me I have not attempted to open it or peek inside in any way. I think the three of us, Richard, privately thought about what it may contain but by agreement we have not shared our thoughts with each other and you start with no dis-advantage."

"Oh, get on with it Dad." Said Sian, "No long speeches, It is not the Rotary club dinner!"

"Thank you Peter, I never doubted it for a second." Richard smiled at his host.

"It will probably be a damp squib!" said Tom, gloomily

"Has anyone told you that sometimes you are an absolute Eeyore?" Sian asked him.

CHAPTER THIRTY-ONE

Winchester Hospital
Hampshire

24th October 2017

By hand; to be opened by Addressee only

My Dear Peter,
I am aware that this is the last letter I shall write. I know that and no amount of medical wisdom will tell me otherwise.

It is therefore with extreme care that I put pen to paper. In one sense I suppose I should say this is for your eyes only and yet you have told me before that you have friends in whom you have complete trust and I am content to rely on your discretion and wisdom. You have not at any stage let me down and I know that you will not do so now.

I have no family living that I acknowledge. No siblings, no children, few friends. I mention this not because of loneliness or to complain but for you to understand that in every way this letter acts as a closure. I would not want to prompt you into taking any action because of it; I would not wish it and there is no need.

As I think you may have realised I have used your kind offices to clear the decks, as it were, from all the secrets and falsehoods I have lived with over so many years and by this letter I hope to complete the task. It is selfish of me, of course, but I know you will understand and the empathy between us renders this task so much easier.

I told you that Freddy disappeared from our lives that night. He trashed Olly's house and left, never to return. We knew he was injured but even I could only guess at how bad it was. I was left to look after Olly as best as I could, but it soon became clear that the emotional impact of it all had tipped him over the edge into what was the start of dementia.

I know we should have sought professional help but we had both been living a life of lies and cover ups and I could see no way out of it at that time. So I did the best I could while Olly's dementia was still in its early stages. He had moments of clarity and I seized those moments to plan for the future, or what was left of it. Olly could not, and would never, get over the treachery of Freddy. It was the source of his whole existence.

While we were still living in the company house I decided that perhaps the best way to solve his depression was to mark Freddy's departure in a way that would demand that Olly accepted the fact that Freddy had gone and so encourage him to look forward and not back. I hit on the idea of a gravestone that marked the period when Olly and Freddy had lived together and shared some happier times. It was a silly idea, perhaps, but we put the gravestone at the foot of a tree in the garden of the house. Of course once Olly was forced to give up the house and move to the flat we had no place to put it.

Olly's condition was worsening by then but I persuaded him that we should put it in an out of the way spot at the churchyard; so he could visit it now and again.

Somehow between us we managed to get it in the back of the car and to the churchyard without anyone seeing. To answer your next question Peter, there is no body beneath the stone. There is no point in looking.

I think that is all I want to say. You may well have further questions but I will of course not be here to answer them. I can do nothing to help Olly now as he is in a twilight zone of his life.

Thank you, Peter, for being there.

Amy."

Richard, Tom and Sian shifted in their seats uneasily, uncomfortable at what they had heard, unsure whether to feel relief or sadness at the way Amy had achieved closure.

"There is nothing else for us to do then. It is the end of the trail and I am not sure if we should be proud or ashamed or ourselves." said Tom, summarising the mood which had settled on the four of them.

"No," Richard added, "it is an extraordinary story and all very sad.

At least there is no one else who can be hurt and as Amy says, it brings closure."

Peter looked up from the papers in front of him. "That was not the end of the letter. There is a postscript and I am not sure you will want to hear it. I have glanced at it whilst you were talking, but having heard this much I think I have got to read it to you, regardless."

He looked at all the puzzled faces before him until Richard said, "Of course you must, Peter."

*   *   *

"P.S.
Peter,

I have read my own letter over and over again and decided that in some ways it is inadequate. I have found it very difficult to relive the events of the past and what I have told you so far is incomplete. I owe it to you to deal with these omissions however hard that may be for me.

You asked me once whether I believed Olly when he said Freddy had slipped and accidentally fallen on the knife. I wanted to believe Olly but to this day I am not sure.

I said we did not see Freddy again after he had trashed the house and left. That is not true. Some days later Olly was asleep upstairs and I answered the door to Freddy with a coat flung over his wounded shoulder, half crazed, or so it seemed. He was clearly very ill, probably from blood infection and he started shouting at me. Suddenly it was all too much; to my mind he had destroyed my only chance of marrying the man I loved; he had thrown all our kindness and generosity back into our faces. He had effectively destroyed Olly's life and here he was demanding even more from us both. I lost control; I wanted to punish him in every way possible for what he had done. I grabbed a kitchen knife and I screamed at him and ran at him like the mad woman I was. I lunged at him again and again; on his shoulder, at his hands, on his arms, anywhere I could reach.

Then I opened the front door and physically threw him outside, not knowing or caring what I had done. The last I saw of him he was stumbling down the garden path.

The rest is true; we did not ever see him again and to this day I have no idea what happened to him.

Medically I doubt whether he could have survived for long. In my eyes I had killed him and I have lived with that for the rest of my life.

There really is nothing more to say now Peter. I have already paid for my crime a hundred times over.

Once again, and finally, goodbye.
Amy"

CHAPTER THIRTY-TWO
EPILOGUE

Oliver Brady died from pneumonia some three weeks later in hospital and was buried in the village cemetery. With the Church's permission the headstone to Freddy was removed and buried with Olly in his grave. Freddy's fate remained a mystery.

Tom Wakefield started his course on Husbandry, in due course graduated and bought a smallholding to the south of Winchester.

Peter Jordan expanded his practice and entered into a joint partnership with a younger doctor. He maintained his own private practice for a limited number of villagers and was able to restrict his workload and to enjoy the benefits of semi-retirement.

Maxence Moreau was arrested by the DGSI, dismissed for gross dereliction of duties and tried for conspiracy to murder and numerous offences under the Official Secrets Act. He was sentenced to fifteen years' imprisonment. François Duval was the main prosecution witness.

Geoffrey Dawson retired the following year from MI5 receiving a substantial pension and a minor award from the Honours Committee. He was succeeded by Neil Pearce, while Bill Smithson resumed his normal duties and faded into the background.

François Duval made a good recovery from his injuries and was granted a six month sabbatical by DGSI to convalesce. He travelled to England at Richard's invitation and stayed with him, renewing their close friendship. They went on lengthy country walks that inevitably ended up at a pub, reliving their past and discovered a shared sense of humour that re-introduced a perspective to each of their lives. Towards the end of François' visit Sian would accompany them, infrequently at first but more regularly as time went on. Richard diplomatically discovered reasons why he could no longer join them.

Sian Jordan was captivated by François; his accent, his laughter and his looks. She soon recognised that he was a skilled Lothario and that there would have been many before her who had fallen for his charms, but in truth she did not really care. Nonetheless she was at pains to set up artificial barriers between them, to refuse invitations and call on all her past experiences to create uncertainty. They were quite possibly falling in love but neither fully understood the other, nor where it was leading.

Richard Merrington revived his relationship with his daughter, Jan. They revisited their favourite Chinese restaurant and shared confidences, just as they had in the past. She could see that her father was tired but some days he visibly relaxed.

He was delighted to see François again and over the weeks worry seemed to ease out of Richard's very being. He busied himself in village life and only occasionally thought about the future that lay ahead of him. He now enjoyed the country life and the people and he made more friends than he had ever known. He became content and happy and it showed. Until, that is, he received a message on his answer-phone.

> *"Richard, is that you?" You may remember me. My name is Neil Pearce. Do you think we could meet up some time? I have come across a situation where I think you could help! Do give me a ring on the number you already have."*

*   *   *